I0708760

A Valentine Anthology

A COLLECTION OF ROMANTIC SHORT STORIES

BY

ALICE CLAYTON
JENNIFER DELUCY
NICKI ELSON
JESSICA MCQUINN
VICTORIA MICHAELS
ALISON OBURIA

OMNIFIC PUBLISHING
DALLAS

Omnific Publishing
P.O. Box 793871, Dallas, TX 75379
www.omnificpublishing.com

First Omnific ebook edition, February 2010
First Omnific trade paperback edition, February 2010

The characters and events in this book are fictitious.
Any similarity to real persons, living or dead,
is coincidental and not intended by the author.

Library of Congress Cataloguing-in-Publication Data

Clayton, Alice; DeLucy, Jennifer; Elson, Nicki; McQuinn, Jessica; Michaels, Victoria; Oburia, Alison
A Valentine Anthology/Alice Clayton, Jennifer DeLucy, Nicki Elson,
Jessica McQuinn, Victoria Michaels, Alison Oburia– 1st ed.
ISBN 978-1-936305-15-5
1. Valentine's Day—Fiction. 2. Romance—Fiction.
3. Anthology—Fiction. I. Title

10 9 8 7 6 5 4 3 2 1

Book Design by Barbara Hallworth

Printed in the United States of America

*A
Valentine
Anthology*

TABLE OF CONTENTS

With a Double Oven
Alice Clayton

"Looks like it's just you and me, kiddo." I nodded sadly as I looked around the empty house. Pillows arranged artfully, furniture placed just so, colors on the walls chosen with attention to detail bordering on the psychotic. My home was beautiful. My home was perfect.

My home was lonely. I wandered from room to room with Mary Jane at my heels, looking at pictures in frames, adjusting magazine stacks, brushing a bit of dust that was almost imaginary from the top of a lamp. I surveyed my quiet world. Sighing loudly, it echoed through the space, and I walked towards the kitchen to make myself a lunch.

Mary Jane nosed at my hand as I made a turkey sandwich, asking if she too could share in my lunch. Her big brown eyes blinked up at me, giving me her best "gimme" face.

"Silly girl, you eat better than almost any dog I know," I said, placing a piece of turkey where she could reach it. She licked my fingertips, smiled her doggie smile, and inhaled it in one bite. I smiled down at her, letting my fingertips now tangle in her soft brown hair, thinking of a very different Valentine's Day.

"Timothy, what the hell did you do?" I cried, spying the cardboard box with telltale air holes punched through the sides.

"Just open it. Don't analyze it, just open it." He laughed, nudging it towards me.

"Are you crazy? Whatever is inside that box, we can't afford it!" I warned, approaching the box.

"Maddie, sometimes you just have to say, 'I want this,' ya know? Besides, once we're married and I'm a big time lawyer, we will be rolling in it. Now, open it before it opens itself." He laughed as the package began to shake. Rolling my eyes at his impractical gift, I approached it and could hear whining from inside. My heart immediately began to melt as I tore the top off the box and gazed inside.

There, perched on top of an old towel, was the sweetest little puppy I had ever seen. Black, with a brown stripe and white breast, the puppy yipped at us as Timothy and I peeked over the top.

"I can't believe you did this," I said softly, already in awe as I picked up the puppy, which promptly licked my face.

"Well, I thought you might like some company on the nights I have to work late," he whispered in my ear as I cuddled the puppy to me.

"We really can't afford this, but somehow I'm not thinking about that right now." I giggled as I kissed my new friend.

"What will you name her?" he asked

"It's a her? Oh, I always wanted a girl!" I squealed as I set her down to explore her new home. We watched as our new charge investigated the tiny apartment, becoming fascinated with the dish-towel that was hanging from the oven. We both laughed as she pulled it down on top of herself, and then barked and looked back at us expectantly.

"Mary Jane," I whispered suddenly.

"Mary Jane what?"

"Mary Jane. That's what we are naming her."

"Awfully old lady for a tiny puppy, don't you think?" He frowned.

"That's why it's funny!" I protested, picking up Mary Jane and delighting in the feel of her soft fur against my cheek.

"Mary Jane it is. Happy Valentine's Day, Maddie," he murmured in my ear, wrapping his arms around my waist and pulling me back tight against his chest.

"Happy Valentine's Day to you, sweetie. I love you," I whispered back, as the three of us cuddled close.

Ten years, a wedding, a house, and a successful law career later, and now I was spending Valentine's Day alone. I snorted as I dumped the rest of my sandwich down the drain, losing my appetite as I looked again at the note scrawled on the blackboard by the back door.

Having dinner tonight with the partners, don't wait up for me.
Tim

Is it possible to know, to pinpoint exactly when romance dies? As I sat in my lovely home, surrounded by my lovely things, I found myself wishing for the days when we had nothing *but* love, when we'd made sure we experienced love as often as possible.

$\backsim$

"Sweetie, what smells so good?"

"You mean besides me?" I giggled, turning from the stove and smiling over my shoulder at my new husband, noticing the circles under his eyes, the way he hung up his trench coat as though it weighed fifty pounds. Everyone warned that the first year at the firm would be the hardest, and they were right. Eighty hours a week Tim was working, and we barely saw each other. The money that everyone foolishly thinks young lawyers make had yet to start rolling in, although I did the best I could to make our little apartment feel as homey as I could.

"You always smell amazing, babe, but what's that you're cooking?" he asked, snuggling into me from behind and wrapping his arms around me. His chin perched on my shoulder as I stirred the sauce.

"I splurged. Tonight you get meat sauce with actual meat on your pasta." I laughed as he snuck an artichoke heart from the salad I had made.

"Wow, and artichoke hearts! I don't think we've had those since our wedding." He laughed back, kissing my neck in the way that always made my knees weak.

"I figured hearts were appropriate today," I whispered as he made his way down my neck and gave me tiny kisses across the top of my back and shoulders.

"Very appropriate," he murmured. *"Where's that little milk bottle you picked up at the antique show?"*

"Under the sink. Why?" I asked, feeling the loss of his body as he pulled away from me. I turned to see him taking the bottle out and placing a single pink and a single red tulip into the bottle.

"Sweetie, they're beautiful." I grinned, loving that I had a husband who remembered my fondness for tulips. Roses were easy; tulips were special.

"You're beautiful," he answered, brushing my hair back so he could kiss on my neck a little more easily.

"You're cheesy, but I'll forgive you if you keep doing that." I moaned as I felt his teeth begin to nibble on my neck.

"Happy Valentine's Day, babe," he said in my ear, making me smile at the sauce.

"Right back atcha," I whispered, dropping the spoon as he spun me around to kiss me fully.

Having never managed to burn a meat sauce before, I wasn't even aware that it could be done. But, an hour and several orgasms later, as we pulled ourselves off the kitchen floor, disheveled and wearing no clothes, the sauce was a reddish brown nightmare. The pasta no longer had actual shapes, but was rather a blob of cream colored mush.

Valentine's Day dinner that year turned into hastily delivered Chinese food, which we ate naked, perched on a blanket on the middle of the floor. We drank ginger ale out of our champagne flutes that were a wedding present. It looked the same as the expensive stuff.

Why did we eat our dinner naked on the middle of the floor? Because we were newlyweds, and we could.

I remembered that particular Valentine's Day fondly as Mary Jane and I ran at the park. It's so easy when you're young and crazy in love to make everything romantic. It became more difficult, as the years went on, to make it a priority.

I worked when Tim and I were first married. I'd graduated with a degree in English Lit, but worked for a catering company while he was in law school. I found that I really enjoyed baking, and as I learned more and more about the catering business, I began to make a name for myself with my old-fashioned cakes. Mounded high with frosting and multiple layers, I specialized in cakes that people remembered from their childhood: rich walnut-fudge, snowy coconut, thick red-velvet. They became quite popular, and I considered going into business for myself.

But, after Tim began working at the firm, we were sure we would be starting a family soon. Once he was making enough money for us to buy our first little starter home, I gave up my job and threw myself full time into setting up house and…ahem…family planning. We had a lot of fun trying to get pregnant, although after a year or so of trying and no luck, I asked my doctor to run a few tests. We knew soon enough that children were not going to be possible for us, and we put family plans on hold while we decided what we wanted out of our life. We settled into a nice rhythm, and realized that we were pretty damn happy with just the two of us, with Mary Jane as our pseudo-child.

By this time, Tim had begun to work his way up in the firm. We were able to purchase a newer, larger home, and as the years began to go by, the thoughts I had about running my own business faded away as I enjoyed the role of homemaker. I volunteered, I gardened, and I enjoyed my life. Sometimes people looked down on women who devoted their lives to creating a wonderful home, but I was proud of the home I had helped make for the two of us, and proud of my life.

It wasn't until the last year or so, when Tim began working even harder to make partner, that I started to feel lonely and a little obsolete. I began baking again, at first just for friends when they raved about something I had brought to a garden party, but then began to get asked to bake for children's parties, or someone's going-away party, and before I knew it, women were placing orders. I had been considering talking to Tim about trying to make a go at the catering business for a while now, and him forgetting Valentine's Day was perfect ammunition.

When I pulled into the driveway, I noticed Tim's car was already in the garage. I looked at my watch. It was only 5:30, and he was never home this early. Most nights, I was lucky to get dinner on the table for him before eight.

Mary Jane and I walked in through the kitchen, and even she was sniffing the air as though something was odd. I saw his trench coat slung across the back of the chair, but no Tim. I listened for him…nothing.

"Timothy?" I called out, and then I heard a muffled "Ow!" from upstairs. Maybe he did remember it was Valentine's Day after all, but I knew better than to get my hopes up. He had been so busy lately working on a new case; he was on track to make partner, and the hours he was working were becoming ridiculous. When his mind was on work, his mind was on work.

Our marriage was a good one, but more and more lately I was feeling that work was coming first, and I missed having my husband at home. When he was first out of law school, the hours were expected. And we worked around it; even as newlyweds we found time to...well...connect. But lately?

There had been no…connecting…at all for weeks, and I was starting to get a little nervous.

"Ow!" I heard again from upstairs, and Mary Jane and I went to check it out. Maybe he was home early just to surprise me, maybe we could "connect" after all. Maybe we could….

I stopped myself before my brain could get too carried away, as it would only lead to disappointment if he hadn't remembered. I walked upstairs, calling out to let him know I was home.

"Sweetie, what are you doing up there?" I cried, as Mary Jane raced ahead to say hello. The two of them were pretty funny together, and even she missed the long runs they used to go on.

"Maddie? Hey, I'm in the bedroom," he called back, and I made my way towards our room. He was in the closet, pushing past suit after suit, obviously looking for something.

"Hey, babe, what are you doing home?" I asked, leaning in for a quick kiss. He popped his head back out of the clothing to kiss me quickly, giving me a glance at his blue eyes and curly blond hair before disappearing back into the suits.

"Needed to pick up something for dinner, have you seen my blue tie? The one you got me for Christmas two years ago?" he asked, still digging.

"Here, why are you changing ties?" I asked, reaching thru the mess he was making and selecting the tie almost without having to look for it. It was my favorite; the blue was the exact color of his eyes, deep, almost indigo. Elizabeth Taylor would be jealous if she ever got a peek at my husband's peepers.

"Eh, I dragged my tie through some soup at lunch today, and I can't very well go out to such an important dinner with a soupy tie, now, can I?" He chuckled as he took the tie from me, unbuttoning his top button and slipping his old tie off. He handed it to me, and I threw it into the dry-cleaning pile, irritated all over again that he was still planning on going out for dinner.

I stomped back into the bedroom and sat down on the bed with a huff, wondering if I should even bring it up or not. He worked hard, and he worked hard so that we could enjoy the spoils of a good life. But forgetting Valentine's Day?

"What are you doing for dinner, babe?" he asked, heading into the bathroom. I could hear the water running.

"I didn't really make any plans. I was sort of waiting," I hinted. Mary Jane was sitting in the closet doorway, her head turning right to left as we talked, like she was watching a tennis match.

"What's that?" he yelled back, the running water making it difficult for him to hear.

"I said, 'I didn't really make any plans. I was sort of waiting!" I yelled, laying back against the pillows and trying hard to bite back tears. I turned my face away from the bathroom door, punching at the pillow like a little girl about to throw a tantrum. And if he asked me one more time what I was doing for dinner, I may have thrown more than that.

The water stopped in the bathroom, and I could hear him fumbling around.

"Sorry, babe, water was running. Now what did you say?" he asked, and I could feel my fist clench. I rose up on one elbow, preparing to unleash hell.

"I said, you forgetful forgetful man, that—" I swung around on the bed to see him standing in the doorway.

Holding a handful of tulips. Red and pink tulips.

"What the…" I exclaimed as he crossed the room towards me.

"You really thought I had forgotten what today is, didn't you? Silly woman." He laughed as I perched on the side of the bed, my expression confirming his statement.

"But you said…and your note said…and… what?" I asked, my thoughts confused and whirling as he sat down on the bed next to me and smoothed my hair back from my face. Handing me the bouquet, he placed his hands on either side of my face and kissed me. Long. Deep. Intense.

"I love you, and I'm taking my best girl out for dinner tonight. So get dressed." He grinned, kissing me once more just below my right ear, knowing that had always been the spot that made me blush.

"Yes, and I'm taking my other best girl out right now, yes, yes I am!" he called to Mary Jane as she leapt to her feet at the word "out."

I clutched my flowers as I sat on the bed, watching my beautiful husband leave our bedroom. Mentally, I began running through the dresses in my closet, and I knew I had just the thing for tonight….

❦

I pushed back from the table and patted my tummy appreciatively.

"That was the single best meal of my entire life." I sighed, taking another sip of my wine.

Tim had taken me to our favorite little Spanish restaurant, and we feasted like there was no tomorrow. Grilled shrimp, mussels steamed with chorizo, tiny veal and pork meatballs with Manchego cheese, followed by a pan of paella—it was shocking how much food we had consumed. I'd also had glass upon glass of sparkling Cava and was now working my way through a lovely little glass of port.

"It was good, but I don't think anything compares to the mangoes I ate off your tummy in Bora Bora last year," he murmured, meeting my eyes over the rim of his glass as he finished off his own after-dinner drink.

"Hmm, yes, that was rather nice. OK, vacation meals aside, this was pretty great." I sighed, stretching out my legs and inadvertently rubbing his leg with my foot.

"You trying to play footsie, Mrs. Foster?"

"I wasn't planning on it, Mr. Foster, but now that you mention it," I teased back, nudging my shoe off and running my toes up inside his pant leg. He closed his eyes at the contact and smiled.

"Don't start something you can't finish," he warned, opening his eyes and gazing across the table with darkened eyes.

"Who says I can't finish it?" I smirked, running my foot up higher into his lap.

"Will there be anything else?" our waiter asked, appearing at the table at the perfect time.

"My goodness, no, this dinner was perfect." I sighed again, letting my foot drop back down to my discarded shoe and sliding back into it. As I looked around the restaurant, I noticed once again all the happy couples. Valentine's Day was certainly a manufactured holiday, but a holiday that celebrated love? I wasn't complaining.

"Thank you, I think we're ready for the check." Tim nodded.

"Yes, more than ready," I whispered, noticing the way his eyebrows rose.

"Is that so?"

"Mm-hmm." I nodded, winking.

"Good to know, babe." He winked back.

Moments later we were ensconced in his car, speeding home. His hand had taken up residence on my left knee, and he was making tiny circles with his fingertips, driving me crazy.

"You really thought I forgot about tonight, didn't you?" he said suddenly.

"Yes," I admitted.

"I thought for sure you were gonna see right through the 'having dinner with the partners' thing. I just wanted to surprise you."

"I know, sweetie. It's just that we…well…we haven't had a lot of time for ourselves lately. For quite awhile, actually," I prodded. He clasped my hand and brought it to his lips.

"I miss you," he answered, turning to look at me now while we waited for the light to change.

"I miss you, too," I breathed, feeling tears prick at my eyes as I gazed at the only man I had ever truly loved. The only man that still made my skin shiver at his touch. The only man that would ever know me as well as he did, and the only man that I would love the rest of my life. "Take me home," I whispered, bringing his hand to my lips now, kissing and loving him.

"And then what?" he teased, eyes back on the road as we drove through the night.

"Then you can just take me," I teased back, my head falling backwards against the headrest as he stepped on the gas a little more forcefully.

I giggled, adoring the fact that I could still affect my husband so.

~

We made our way up the stairs, not turning lights on or off, too impatient to get to our room. Tim's suit coat hung from the front door, my shoes were discarded somewhere in the living room, and my stockings were now hanging from the banister.

"What the hell kind of knot did you tie in this?" he grumbled, fighting with the bow in my red silk wrap dress. We were momentarily delayed on the landing, hands frantic and mouths crashing greedily. Mary Jane had wisely retreated to her doggie bed in the kitchen.

"Are you really going to let a simple knot stand in your way, big guy?" I chuckled, pressing my mouth against his ear and nibbling lightly, something that drove him crazy.

"Oh, Maddie, I really did love this dress," he answered darkly, pulling me back so he could look me in the eye. I felt a tug and then a cool breeze as he shredded my dress around me. I inhaled sharply and then stared at my husband, both of us breathing heavily. I raised an eyebrow at him, and that was all he needed.

He attacked.

Lifting me off my feet, he wrapped my legs around his waist and carried me up the rest of the stairs before I knew what was happening. He ran me down the hallway, knocking back and forth off the walls like a pinball as we laughed.

"You gonna make it to the bedroom there, Mr Foster?" I teased, as he pinballed off another corner and banged my hip into the doorway.

"You got something against hallway floors, Mrs. Foster?" he warned, and he let his grip slip just enough that I began to slide down his body.

"No!" I cried, and he smirked as he swung me back up.

"Bedroom it is," he answered, and threw me like a sack of potatoes onto the bed.

"Oof! That was romantic," I grumbled as I looked down at my tangled limbs and tattered dress.

"I am getting to the romantic part, babe," he murmured, unfastening his tie and dragging it slowly through his shirt collar.

"Oh my," I said, and a slow grin crossed his face.

"You really are a sucker for this tie, aren't you?" he chuckled, letting it fall on the end of the bed as he began working on his cufflinks.

"Yep, it's the blue," I admitted, feeling slow warmth spread over my body as I gazed at my husband. He was as beautiful as the day we met, as beautiful as the day he proposed to me.

"Have you seen my keys?"

"Nope, not since you came in. They aren't on the table by the door?"

"No, I already checked there. Will you check my coat pocket, I'm gonna check in the bedroom," he called out as he walked down the hallway. I grumbled to myself. Tim was always losing his keys, and our reservation was for 7:30. There was no way the restaurant would hold a table for us if we were late, not on Valentine's Day.

His trench coat was lying across one of the chairs in the living room, two feet from the coat tree I had placed by the front door. I had asked him again and again to hang up his coat when he came in, but I still hung it up for him most evenings. I thrust my hand into the pockets, moving towards the door as I searched for his keys. My hand ruffled through bits of paper, Tic Tacs, and grasped a...small velvet box?

I pulled it from his pocket, hearing the floor creak behind me. I turned, already speechless, to see Tim on one bended knee, smiling hopefully at me.

"What are you doing?" I whispered, tears already flowing down my cheeks.

"Proposing?" he whispered back, reaching out to take the box from my trembling hand and opening it towards me. I gasped as

I saw the perfectly round, perfectly me diamond sparkling back at me.

"Oh, Timothy, yes yes yes!" I shouted, throwing my arms around his neck and hugging him tightly. So tightly that I toppled us both and we rolled in the direction of the kitchen.

Laughing wildly, we came to rest in the doorway, and he exclaimed, "Now, I didn't exactly ask you yet," as he placed the ring on my finger. "Maddie, I couldn't love you more. Be my wife?" he asked earnestly, nibbling on his lower lip the way he did when he was nervous. Or hungry. But tonight I was guessing nervous.

"Can I say yes now?" I asked, gazing at the ring twinkling brightly on my hand.

"Yes!" he shouted, and I shouted back, "Yes yes yes!"

We clutched at each other, hugging tightly and kissing any part of each other we could reach without letting go.

We missed our reservation that Valentine's Day.

Tim was making his way up the bed from the bottom. In my musings on Valentine's Days past, I had missed most of his little strip show and now gazed down at him: his tousled blond hair, blazing blue eyes, and body as trim as the day we met. He was still stunning, and he began to sweep kisses from right knee to left. I watched his hand grasp my thigh. His wedding band looked wonderful against my skin.

"Timothy?"

"Yeah, babe?"

"I love you," I said simply, dropping my hand and raising his chin so he was looking directly at me.

"I love you too, Maddie," he answered back, turning his face into my hand and kissing my palm. "More than you will ever know."

He continued to kiss my palm, and I let my other hand come up to run my fingers through his hair.

"Timothy?"

"Yeah, babe?"

"Can you take off the rest of this dress?"

He stopped kissing my hand and smirked up at me. "I'm on it," he winked.

The dress was removed, leaving bits of red silk strewn across the bed and both nightstands. The rest of his clothes soon joined them, albeit in better shape than the dress.

Tim was poised above me, his body strong and lean and perfect. My legs wrapped around his waist, and he smiled as he slipped inside me, slowly, gently, intensely. I sighed as I felt him.

Even after all these years, there is still that moment when we are together again that makes me sigh. I hope I never lose that sigh.

As we moved together, dancing our dance that we have done so many times before, but which always feels new and different and spectacular, I was reminded once more of my love for him. I knew my house would never feel lonely again.

And later, when we were snuggled together, arms and legs wrapped around each other as tightly as they could be, I sighed again, feeling pure contentment.

"I missed you," I whispered, cradling him to my breast. Our chests rose and fell together, his weight on me wanted and wholly necessary.

"Well, soon you won't miss me as much," he said, his voice muffled by my neck where his mouth was continuing to place tiny, sweet kisses.

"What does that mean?" I asked quietly, my fingers weaving shapes and patterns on his back.

"Oh, I didn't tell you? I made partner. I can finally slow down a little."

I froze, and consequently he froze. Seconds later, I began to beat on him with a pillow.

"You made partner! You little shit! How long have you know about this?" I yelled, forgetting that I was naked and yet still brandishing a throw pillow like a serious weapon. He laughed, trying to dodge me, and knelt on the bed in front of me, grabbing both of my hands to stop the attack.

"A few days ago, but I wanted to wait and tell you on Valentine's Day." He laughed, noticing that now that I had stopped the assault, I was taking in what this would mean.

More time at home. Less weekends working. Dinner actually at 6:30, maybe even 6:00. And more money.

"Babe? What're you thinking about?" he asked, moving closer to me on the bed and crushing his naked body against my own.

"A Viking stove with a double oven."

"A Viking what?" he asked, coaxing me back down onto the bed with him. I perched on top of him, legs on either side. He loved this view of me, and I knew how good I looked.

"A Viking stove with a double oven. That money is gonna come in real handy."

"You want to buy a new stove? We just remodeled the kitchen....Mmm, babe, what are you doing there?" he stuttered as I began to move above him. My husband? He had great recovery time.

"Every good caterer needs a Viking stove." I smirked, watching as his eyes grew wider.

"Caterer? A Viking stove?"

"With a double oven. Happy Valentine's Day, Timothy," I said, as he sat up underneath me and things began to happen down below.

"Happy…Valentine's…Day, …babe…. Mmm."

Magnus of Pfelt, Conquering Viking Lord
Jennifer DeLucy

It had begun with an unhealthy fixation, with days spent thinking of him, drawing his image again and again in a mental portrait. I couldn't leave him behind, couldn't leave him where he rightly belonged. And so, regardless of my self-acknowledged foolishness, evening could scarcely come too soon, because the evening meant dreams, and that's when he showed himself.

You don't ever expect to fall in love with words. No one can anticipate such a thing. But should it happen, God help you, because it will seem that no existent man is enough; none can equal what you have perfected in your mind.

As I remember, the phrases set themselves on the page. Penning them never felt like a chore—more a forceful obsession, an urge to the point of discomfort that would not be neglected. Twelve years I'd labored, bowed over a keyboard…twelve years in writing these novels, and none of them had ever held me as captive, droopy-eyed, and fading into the wee hours of the night as this.

In the past, though, I had written for everyone else. I'd composed what I knew to be a valuable escape for the troubled, for those who sought a new perception or means of inspiration. But now, I was writing for my own devices, and what had begun as a well-intentioned dose of self-indulgence had turned into something bigger than even I could control.

I'd attempted, in the beginning, to place the blame elsewhere. I told myself that it was all *his* doing—this horrific character of a man that any self-respecting, strong-minded woman would have loathed for his chauvinism and savagery. But my neurosis was mine to own. I had created it, nurtured it, and I was drawn to those very things that reason begged I despise—to that booming voice, the over-built, over-sexed fiend whose presence few but his author could abide. It seemed I could no longer tell fact from fantasy, and moreover, that knowledge simply didn't matter anymore. I was in too deep, and as I wrote it, so he was: perfect.

The answering machine had, for weeks now, ceased to serve a purpose. It was full to brimming with calls that would not be returned. Even my fiancé had given up on me. Poor Peter, a thousand miles away. If he only knew. The man just couldn't measure up when compared to Magnus. Peter's imperfections, his tiring emotional needs, all the baggage that came with a real relationship, felt more troublesome than rewarding. And shall I even mention the sex? Hell, with Peter it was hit or miss. He had tried, bless him. And sometimes he succeeded. But it was hardly guaranteed, and who wanted to be disappointed? So, I'd become a recluse of my own making. I'd allowed the world to fall away so that I could live in a dream. Tonight, Magnus would ask me to stay, as he always did. And this time, I'd determined to say yes. This time, I would not return to the binds of sanity.

The alarm on my bedside table read ten p.m. It was quite a bit earlier than my usual bedtime, but patience had never been my strong suit. Clothed only in a light nightgown, I lay atop the bed, hardly disrupting a pillow, and waited for sleep to come.

It didn't.

Unconsciousness was dawdling tonight, causing me to toss and turn. I cursed my own reluctant psyche. Perhaps my sanity was fighting back. Well, I'd show it! No good soldier goes to battle without a weapon.

I reached over and opened the top drawer of my table and pulled out a bottle of sleeping pills, dumping one into my palm and swallowing it dry. That would take care of the issue.

Soon enough, a black veil, heavier than could be resisted, lowered the lids of my eyes, and when next I opened them, I found myself in a great hall made of towering wooden planks with golden, fierce-eyed creatures etched into the beams. Lights flickered orange from the many torches posted to the walls, and they cast dancing shadows along the floor and ceiling. Beneath me was a thick, lush rug of animal hair. He had laid it there, knowing I would return.

There was to be a raucous celebration tonight. I knew it, because I had written it.

Just as the thought emerged, I heard the nearby music. These songs, heady, triumphant, and ancient, would have been unfamiliar to the world I'd left behind, but I had been here several times, so I pressed my hands into the warm fur and pushed myself up, following the folk horns down the corridor to their source.

There in the vast door frame I stood, watching as he laughed, surrounded by warriors and their women. His blond hair poured over broad, massive shoulders, half-hiding the burned-on symbols of forcibly gotten gain. I considered the lives he had callously taken, the many lands his men had conquered and set ablaze in his name. The breadth of his destruction was monstrous, and I knew this well. I had been there when he ran them all through. I had composed every scene, counted the bodies, written of the aftermath. And yet, as I watched him, his brown eyes gleaming with pride, the face ever handsome as it was glorified in contentment, I believed I loved him.

As if sensing me there, he looked up and smiled broadly. Then he rose from his place while everyone gazed on, awe-struck as usual at his unorthodox conduct. It was understood, you see, that Magnus of Pfelt, Conquering Viking Lord, stood for no man, let alone a woman.

He came to me quickly, leaving the others behind. "The Gods have delivered you to my side once again," he said, towering above me like a tree.

"Yes." I nodded.

"And you are radiant as the sun. What do you smell of this night?"

"Escada." I smirked, knowing he wouldn't possibly understand.

"A beautiful word. Is it a flower?" he asked.

"It's…well…no. It's hard to explain," I said.

"Ah, well. This is of no importance," he added, satisfied with not knowing. "You will come to my bed tonight. I shall make you sing."

I had blushed the first time Magnus spoke those lines to me. But now I remembered they were coming, so I was spared the embarrassing display of feminine vulnerability. Certainly, it was my own fault, since I'd written him to speak in such an overzealously romantic manner, but still—there was no changing it now.

Though I was quite familiar with his castle, he picked me up—as was his preference to do—leaving the curious warriors and jealous women to contemplate their small world, and he carried me through the now familiar passageway to his bed-chambers. He set me down on a mountain of fur and lay beside me.

"You know, you don't have to cart me around like that, Magnus. Honestly, I know the way," I said.

"Do you dislike the feel of my arms?" he asked, grinning.

"Er…no. No, I like it quite a lot, thank you. But still. I tell you every time, and every ti—"

"I refuse to hear of this," he interjected, strongly. "You are my concubine, and I will have you as I please."

I sighed. Right. I would have to see if I could break him of that if I intended to remain. But for now…. "How are you tonight?" I asked, reaching up to touch his face.

"My loins crave you well, Allison. I must show you."

I snorted, my cheeks puffing out as I held in laughter and nodded. That line was just as funny every time he said it. And oh, the horror, the guilt. How could I have done such a disservice to the English language as to write something like that? For shame.

Nonetheless, "Show me," I said, and taking hold of my wrist, Magnus moved my hand down to the pelt covering that clothed his middle. When I slipped my fingers beneath it, I could—as was customary—feel *exactly* how…craving…his loins were. Not only was he hard as iron, but also quite well-endowed, like a proper leading male *should* be.

I bit my lip, signaling my eagerness, and he leaned down, covering my mouth with his. What a kisser he was. That tongue was built to exemplify power, masculinity, and it made my legs (among other parts) melt on contact.

His kiss alone had me mightily worked up, so, feeling for the tie that held the cloak around him, I pulled it loose. I'd really become quite the expert at this. In fact, I was just as skilled as any man was at bra removal, thank you kindly.

I stared, shamelessly, as his cloak fell, which he enjoyed.

"Am I not virile? Am I not pleasing to your eye?" he questioned, jutting out his chest proudly. Yes. I had done a splendid job on Magnus's physique.

"You're perfect." I coddled him. "You're just perfect."

He nodded. "I wish to remove this," he said of my clothing, so I sat up, allowing him to lift the nightgown over my head, and I watched as he fingered a hem, fascinated by the strange print, the vibrant colors. "This one is most beautiful of all," he said, and then tossed it to the side in a heap.

"I'm glad you like...uhm...*liked* it." I laughed, glancing at the floor.

"Yes. But I enjoy what lies beneath it much more," he said. He bent to kiss my neck, which was quite pleasant, and as I enjoyed it, I was again grateful that I'd negated the under apparel. In fact, I'd learned through trial and error that Magnus—lacking the fine-skilled coordination required to unclasp a bra strap—became frustrated with undergarments, and it often resulted in clothing items being thrown into the fire.

"Your breasts are more beautiful than the full moon. They enchant me," he said, nuzzling them. I resisted the desire to roll my eyes. The first time he'd spoken those words out loud, it thrilled me no end. The second time it was nice, as well. By the third, I was trying very hard not to laugh... but at this point, I was reduced to smiling.

On the bright side, while genuine Vikings would probably have known (or cared) very little about the assorted methods of pleasing a woman (what with the pillaging and killing being such a diversion from studying the Kama Sutra), Magnus was something else completely. He was whatever I'd made him to be, which meant that he would simply never, ever fail in the areas to which he'd been...assigned, so to speak. It was the rule. Of course, there *was* that *one* little pitfall—the irksome bravado and "I am your master, you must succumb to me" business, but that was just part of the arrangement. In all fairness, I'd done it to myself. It was too late to compose a more modern-minded love interest. I had already decided to stay, hadn't I?

And so, as his lips ravaged—hungrily, eagerly, relentlessly and so forth—the slopes and contours of my body, I had a thought. But first, *wait for it....*

"I desire to enter you," he announced.

Like clockwork.

"Eh…Magnus?" I started.

"Mmm," he said, spreading my thighs.

"Well, I was thinking we could change things a bit; put some variation in our technique."

He looked up, confused. "Unh?"

Oh, dear, too many big words? "Eh, that is, change the way we do things sometimes. You know?"

"No. I do not understand."

"Well, how about this: I'll suggest something different to do, and you follow my lead, okay?"

"*I* follow *you*?" he repeated, eyes narrowing indignantly. "I follow no one!"

Oops! Time to stroke the ego. "Okay, what I mean is, you have the power to do something new to me. Would you try that?"

"Something…new?" he mused.

"Mm-hm. Can I show you?"

He said nothing, just sat up, looking more confused than ever, waiting for me to end the apparent fuse-shortage in his literarily pre-programmed brain.

"Let's try *this*." I demonstrated, turning around so my back faced him. Now, I imagine that genuine Vikings would probably have known (and cared) quite a *lot* about the—for lack of a more delicate term—canine position. But Magnus was not a genuine anything, and so I wiggled my bum enticingly, hoping he would understand. After a moment of fruitless waiting, I turned my head around to find him gaping at me, painfully clueless.

"Here," I sighed, chuckling to myself as I reached for his erection. "Take me from behind."

"Take you?"

"Well, yes. Enter me," I corrected.

"Oh," he said, wide-eyed. "I will try this."

The second he pushed inside, I gave myself a figurative pat on the back. It was fantastic. Maybe this would work out better than I thought. Maybe I could just rewrite him in my head.

Glancing back again, I noted that Magnus was at a total loss for what to do with the top half of his body. While he puzzled over his right hand, he held the other awkwardly at his side. I groaned and took one of them, holding it against my breast and setting the other on my waist so he could support himself, and then I prayed for the best. Fortunately, the best was what I got. He was doing a splendid job. Lord knows, if there was anything Magnus was good at, it was this.

His powerful hips had the thrusting thing down pat, even if he was a little mechanical, and I would soon be close to "singing" for him again. Just a moment more like this and….

"Oops!" I squeaked as he flipped me over onto my back, continuing his entry in the usual missionary position. All imminent feelings of pleasure promptly disappeared, and I frowned below him.

"Magnus, what are you doing?" I asked, less than pleased.

He moaned, continuing his onslaught.

"You were supposed to be taking me from behind, remember?"

"I like this best," he said without stopping.

"You…like this best," I repeated. He wasn't supposed to *like* things, not *really*, anyway. Only what I told him to like, or else, what was the point of creating your man from scratch? Sadly, it appeared that Magnus was set to automatic default.

"This is…the right…way," he grunted, still thrusting with abandon.

For the umpteenth time I sighed. Fine. I enjoyed it like this, too. And he *was* the master and ruler and all that nonsense. So I closed my eyes and went with it, wrapping my legs around him in the normal fashion to obtain maximum depth. Sure enough, his ceaseless motions had me nearing the point of no return when a rather confounded, conflicting thought crossed my mind. It occurred to me that this whole thing was rather like using a very large, very handsome dildo.

And then my heart sank.

Did I really want predictability? Did I want a never-ending routine that, while always resulting in pleasure, never altered, never faltered? Was he even *capable* of failing? And with that question, had I truly believed that the possibility of failure was a bad thing? Wasn't risk the very marrow of life? Never knowing what you were going to get…or how? Never knowing whether it was going to change your entire existence or leave you dejected? What had I been *thinking*? This was all wrong. I couldn't stay here! And, just as I'd solidified the notion, I realized that I'd been oblivious to my own body when a powerful—and for the first time, *unexpected*—orgasm soared through me, and I cried out loud, surprised by its strength. It was an explosive sign. I had sung for Magnus for the last time.

Falling unceremoniously beside me, my sated warrior slung an arm around my waist, pulling me close to his chest.

"Allison," he said, lazily.

"Yes?" I asked, though there was no need for it.

"Stay with me," he whispered.

I exhaled, patting his arm. "Not tonight," I said, and I closed my eyes, waiting for the black.

I woke with a start, sitting up quickly. When I realized where I was, I sighed with relief. Staring out the bedroom door at my shambles of a house, I saw things as they were for the first time in a long while. We've all been there, I'm certain. We've all known that moment when you wake from the fog of whatever transfixion has lulled you to sleep. That moment is incomparable…and intimidating. You ask yourself, what now?

Climbing out of bed, I padded into the living room to stare at my writing desk, at the manuscript that housed *Magnus of Pfelt, Conquering Viking Lord*, along with all my delusions. There was no question what needed to be done.

So, with purpose, I grabbed a lighter and a few logs for the fireplace, tossed them in, and watched the fire grow to a miniature, crackling inferno. Then, I took the pages and, hesitating for only an instant, dropped them in the center of the fire, watching intently as they burned.

Paper turned to ash, the room filled with the cloying smell of smoke, and I deigned that today I would begin a new novel. It would tell the story of a woman who had lost her way, lost her perspective. She would crawl out of the dark and experience herself again, experience the beauty of life. It would be a triumphant piece of work.

Chapter one began as I picked up the telephone and dialed, listening happily to the garish sound of the dial tone. The line rang and rang, and I waited, poised to give up, when—

"Hello?" The voice was groggy.

"Peter? Did I wake you?"

"Uh, yeah," he said. I could hear him shifting around in bed. "But that's okay. Shit, where have you *been*? Why the hell haven't you been answering the phone? Everybody's really worried, Allison."

"I know. I'm sorry. I was…well, you know how it is when you're writing on a deadline. It won't happen again. I promise," I said.

No, it would never happen again.

I Don't Do Valentine's Day
Nicki Elson

"I don't *do* Valentine's Day." That was one of the first things Jason had learned about Victoria. "It's just a manufactured holiday designed to boost sales during the slow winter months. If I want to tell someone I love them, I'll tell them when I want to, not when a conglomeration of corporations tells me to," she'd asserted a mere three weeks into the relationship.

Jason had smiled. "So, do you have any gripes against the birth of our nation that I should know about?" They were on their way to his friend's Fourth of July party.

"I will always celebrate independence." Victoria had smiled and ruffled his sandy blond hair. She adored this twenty-six year old boy for not being put off by her fervid opinions on trivial matters. He may have been two years her junior, but he already seemed to get her better than any of the older guys she'd gone out with. He got her so well, in fact, that eight months later, they were still together and dating exclusively.

It was Valentine's Day. This year's calendar worked out so that the holiday fell on a Thursday, or what Jason and Victoria referred to as "separate day." It was rare for them to spend a

Thursday evening together because that was the night Victoria partook of her guilty pleasure, her favorite reality TV show—a show that Jason did not share a love of—so he usually took the opportunity to indulge in his own guilty pleasure, X-box Live, a hobby Victoria did not share a love of.

Victoria insisted that there was no need to change their mutually beneficial routine just because it happened to be February 14. And so it worked out that they would not even see each other on Valentine's Day.

Victoria couldn't have been more pleased. Neither one of them had said the big "L" word yet, and she certainly didn't want the first time to be forced out of him by the Hallmark holiday. So it was without a regret that she stepped into the office that morning and responded to the receptionist's cheery greeting of "Happy Valentine's Day" with an equally pleasant "Happy Thursday."

By late morning, the flowers and candy grams started rolling in. Victoria watched the parade of overpriced red roses and pink carnations trot past her cubicle with quiet disdain. These bouquets weren't purchased out of genuine affection; they were purchased under duress, and she wanted no part of the charade. She did, however, accept an overpriced chocolate from Margie, her middle-aged co-worker at the cubicle next door.

"Ugh, deese are dewicious," Victoria mumbled, her mouth still half full of chocolate.

"Yup, it's the good stuff." Margie sighed. "Looks like I'll have to perform for the hubby tonight," she added with a wink.

"Oh, so you prostitute yourself for chocolate, do you?" Victoria laughed, licking the tips of her fingers

Margie shrugged. "Not just any chocolates—these are *Belgian* chocolates. So what about you? What's *your* beau got to send you to get some tonight?"

Victoria shook her head. "I don't do Valentine's Day."

"What do you mean you don't *do* Valentine's Day?"

"What I just said. I don't celebrate. This is just another Thursday for us. I don't expect anything from him, and he doesn't expect anything from me."

"Well, you're at least going to go out for a nice dinner or cook him something special, aren't you?" Margie stated more than asked, a look of genuine concern crossing over her features.

"He can have a nice dinner if he wants to, but it won't be with me. We won't be seeing each other tonight."

"Oh, honey!" Margie exclaimed, pulling a chair up next to Victoria and taking her hand gently in hers. "You two broke up? I'm sorry, I feel like such an idiot going on and on about it."

"No! No. We didn't break up. Everything is fine between us, great in fact. I just don't really like Valentine's Day, the way everything feels so forced, and Jason understands, so we're not celebrating. That's all there is to it."

Margie let Victoria's hand slip out of hers as she sat back and observed her through narrowed eyes. "Oh, I get it—you're like the Grinch who stole Valentine's Day. Well, let me tell you something, no one *forced* that chocolate down your throat."

"What, do you want it back? Here, let me see if I can retch it up for you," Victoria joked.

"Keep it," Margie answered crisply. "Just do me a favor and next time I bring my kids into the office, don't tell 'em the truth about Santa Clause, eh?"

"Margie…." Victoria chided, but Margie was up and out of the chair and back at her own desk in a few short moments.

Victoria sighed and shook her head. It was always so hard to make other people understand. She didn't mind them celebrating; she simply chose not to herself. What was the big deal? She wasn't a Valentine's Grinch…was she?

She hadn't always disparaged Valentine's Day. When she was a kid, it was practically her favorite holiday. She loved picking out her Valentines and then signing all of them. And the classroom Valentine's parties were the best. So, when had she gone sour on this supposed celebration of love?

As she sat at her desk and stared blindly at the report she was supposed to be analyzing, she pinpointed exactly when that had happened: February 15, senior year in college. Adam. She'd known from the beginning that he was a campus player, but they'd been making eyes at each other from across the room for months— whether he was with another girl or not—and when he finally asked her out, it just seemed right, like she was the one who was going to change him.

By the time February had rolled around, Victoria felt confident in calling Adam her boyfriend. For two solid weeks she had diligently tied jolly ranchers to a wire hanger, which she'd bent into the shape of a heart, to make him a candy wreath. When she gave it to him on Valentine's night, he told her that he loved it…then he told her that he loved her…and she'd believed him. But the very next day, she caught him with another girl, and when she confronted him and asked him why he'd bothered telling her he loved her, he had defended himself with, "It was Valentine's Day. I had to."

How could Adam even be the same species as Jason? Most girls would probably be impatient if, after eight months of dating, their boyfriends hadn't said the "L" word yet, but Victoria greatly appreciated Jason's reserve. He wasn't going to say it before he really meant it and not before Victoria was ready to hear it.

"Hey, Ebenezer, I've got some more reports for ya," Margie said and tossed a stack of bound papers over the cubicle wall.

"Ebenezer is Scrooge, not the Grinch."

"Same difference."

Trish came walking past and not-so-subtly scanned Victoria's cubicle. "Aw, no flowers yet?" she said with a mock pout.

"She told him he couldn't send any," Margie informed the newcomer.

"I didn't tell him he couldn't," Victoria insisted. "We don't tell each other what we can and can't do. I merely told him that he need not feel obligated, that I don't expect them, but if for God-only-knows what reason he wants to send me flowers, he's free to do so."

"Really?" Margie drawled skeptically, standing up and looking over the cubicle wall. "And what would you do if flowers did arrive? Shove them up the chimney with glee?"

"I might shove 'em up something else," Victoria answered with a threatening eyebrow raised at her sassy co-worker.

"Touché," Margie replied and sat back down to work.

Trish also exited the scene, leaving Victoria to ruminate on exactly what she would do if a bouquet of flowers did happen to arrive from Jason. She'd be irritated for sure. But then, those wouldn't be typical Valentine's flowers, would they? Because he knew Victoria didn't expect them, so he'd be sending them because he wanted to, not because he had to. She unwittingly conjured a vision of a bouquet placed in the empty corner of her desk. Not red, long-stem roses—too cliché. Daffodils, maybe—a sign of the coming spring. Propped in the middle of the arrangement, she envisioned a card with not a heart in sight, simply the words *Just because.* Very simple, very direct, very sweet, very Jason.

She popped into her e-mail thinking she'd send him a quick—non-sentimental, non-gushy—message to let him know she was thinking about him on this typical Thursday. She smiled when she saw that she already had a message waiting from him: *Which one do you like best?* it said, followed by a series of four links.

She wondered what he was up to—sending her links to her favorite love songs, perhaps? Or a selection of cozy bed and breakfasts for a weekend getaway? She hoped she wouldn't have to slap him upside the head the next day for breaking the rules and getting too mushy on the banned holiday. After all, sending love songs and planning getaways weren't part of Jason's usual repertoire. And that was something she liked about him, because this way, on the rare occasion that he did do something romantic, it meant more.

She opened the first link and found herself gazing with confusion on the image of a small, black cabinet. Underneath the picture, it read *Fits up to a 44" plasma screen.* Suddenly, the only person Victoria wanted to slap upside the head was herself. Her boyfriend wasn't sending her love songs; he was looking for a stand for his new TV and wanted her opinion. Duh.

She looked over the choices, replied with the link to her favorite, and signed off with a "V" and a smiley face emoticon. Turning back to the reports on her desk, she tried not to feel the emptiness radiating from the corner of the desk where the phantom flowers had sat. She was doubting herself—had she been wrong to insist on not celebrating? Perhaps another visit to her Valentine's past would reaffirm her position.

She had refused to let Adam be her last romantic Valentine's memory, and so agreed to go out the following year with a guy she wasn't sure about. Shepherd. He was an all right enough guy, but she didn't know him very well, so it put the whole Valentine's Day pressure into hyper-drive. After a nice dinner, they went out barhopping, and everywhere they went, Shepherd had jammed his demanding tongue down Victoria's throat. Normally she'd have no problem pushing the guy off, but she was determined to have a successful date, so she put up with it. It was Valentine's Day; she had to.

Victoria gave a shudder when she thought back to how much saliva she'd exchanged with that aggressive guy she hardly even knew, all for the sake of a manufactured holiday. Worse than the saliva might've been his teeth, which clanked onto hers whenever he opened too wide. It had truly felt as if he was trying to eat her. Another shudder put Shepherd out of her mind.

She pulled one of the new reports off the stack and flipped it open, but soon her mind turned back to Jason. There was nothing forced or unpleasant about his kisses. Kissing Jason was more like melting into him, rather than the wrestling match it had been with Shepherd. Not that Jason didn't ever give her a good tongue thrashing, but he took his time building up to it, and when he got there, *ooh, baby*. Victoria quickly realized that if her objective was to convince herself that she didn't want to see Jason tonight, she'd better put her mind on a new track, so she jerked her attention back to the report.

Victoria had spent the next three Valentine's Days after Shepherd dateless. Not by design; it had just worked out that way. But she relished the freedom of it, and it was during those years that she fully embraced her liberation from the suffocating holiday. She saw it for what it was—not an innocent celebration of love, but a meaningless date that had been commercialized to boost winter sales. And all of that contrived hype made people say and do things they normally wouldn't, as if those heart-shaped candies contained some sort of hallucinogen. It was a lie and Victoria was done with it.

Two years ago, she'd found herself again in a relationship as the unfortunate date approached, but she'd refused to recant all of her gripes against Valentine's Day. Victoria was not a hypocrite and wasn't about to start celebrating the lie again just because she had a gorgeous new boyfriend. Martin.

"You don't do Valentine's Day, or you don't want to do Valentine's Day with me?" Martin had demanded.

"I don't do Valentine's Day," Victoria had clarified. Then she walked her flirtatious fingers up his chest and said, "I will, however, do *you*...but on February fifteenth, not the fourteenth."

"And you've had other guys agree to this before?" he challenged.

"Well, I guess technically you're the first guy that I've asked."

"This is bullshit, Victoria," Martin had snapped, grabbing her wrist before she could tangle her fingers into his thick, black curls. "Either we're a couple and I take you out for Valentine's Day or—"

"Or?"

"Or we're not a couple," Martin finished, dropping her arm.

"Are you kidding me? An ultimatum? Wouldn't it be easier to club me over the head and just drag me out to the restaurant?" Victoria had half shouted, half laughed.

"I'm not joking around. I have a reservation at eight at Vincenzo's. Either you meet me there, or we're done."

Victoria did not take kindly to threats. She understood that her stance was unconventional, but she also knew that she deserved more respect than Martin was giving her. She had honestly expected that her thirty-something boyfriend would be mature enough to see that. Besides, he'd been telling her that he wanted a woman with a strong independent streak, so she felt fully justified when she stood by her ideals and didn't go to the restaurant. He, in return, didn't call. Ever again.

Once more, Victoria had been foiled by Valentine's Day. She was initially shocked and hurt by Martin's stubbornness, but came to see how fortunate she was to learn so early in the relationship how much of a controlling lunatic he was. She knew she was better off without him.

Even still, it was with slight trepidation that she made it clear to Jason two weeks ago that she was dead serious about ignoring the holiday. But he hadn't demanded or challenged or snapped. He'd taken her face in his hands and gently tilted her head so she was looking straight into his penetrating eyes.

Then he'd arched an earnest eyebrow and asked, "Are you sure?"

Victoria had smiled and answered, "I'm absolutely positive."

He understood.

Trish came walking up to Victoria's desk with a potted white tea rose plant with shiny red foil around its base.

"I was up at reception and this delivery came in," Trish chirped.

Potted tea roses. Very unique, very practical, very thoughtful, very Jason.

Trish held her arms out toward Victoria and then pulled them back.

"Psych!" Trish gloated. "These are for Herman."

Trish's grin broadened as she turned and walked away, towards Herman's office, and Victoria stuck her tongue out at her retreating co-worker's back. Meanwhile, a dirty chuckle rumbled from the direction of Margie's desk.

"Back to work, Cratchit," Victoria snarled.

"Sticks and stones," Margie called back, inciting Victoria to pick up the nearest pen and fling it over the cubicle wall.

The work day inevitably came to an end, with no delivery from Jason. As Margie pulled on her coat, she commented, "Well, looks like you have a very obedient boyfriend."

"Not obedient," Victoria corrected. "Just discerning and tolerant."

"Yeah, yeah," Margie crabbed. "Maybe there are flowers waiting for you at home."

Victoria rolled her eyes, but considered that if Jason were to send flowers, he probably would play it subtle and send them to her apartment. She'd rather have them there to enjoy than at her work cubicle, anyhow. But there were no delivery notices from florists when she got home. And no deliveries came while she heated up the rising crust pizza and poured herself a glass of wine. She did, however, get a short text message from him, just saying hi.

Typically, Victoria had a couple of friends over on Thursdays to watch TV with her, but she'd never quite succeeded in bringing them over to the anti-Valentine's dark side, and so they were out on dates. But as long as she had pizza, wine, and her favorite program to keep her company, she was more than satisfied. As the show progressed, the plot thickened and the players scrambled to secure their positions, but in the end, one of them was voted out and walked away. All alone.

She watched the contestant's lonely exit and thought of Jason. Had she voted him out tonight? He'd made it clear that the decision to spend the evening together was all hers, and she'd never even asked him what he wanted. Wow. She was suddenly struck with how incredibly selfish she'd been. Did he want to spend Valentine's Day with her and she'd pushed him away? She got up and snatched her cell phone, poured another glass of wine, and then plopped back onto the couch. She clicked around and pulled up his last text message to see if she could detect any hurt feelings between the lines.

Hi QT hv fun C U tmrw

Naw, he wasn't hurt, just going with the flow. So very Jason. She admired that about him. He rarely got his feathers ruffled, but was always around to soothe hers. She stared down at his message and realized that she hadn't heard his voice today. She *wanted* to hear his voice. She started dialing, but stopped—she would never call him on a typical Thursday night.

"Damn it," she grumbled. She *really* wanted to hear his voice. If she was being honest, she wanted more than that. She wanted to see him. Jason had been popping into her head all day, and each time it was like some sort of gauzy drape in her mind was pulled aside. Jason was everything she admired and wanted in a man: compassionate, direct, honest, practical, thoughtful, undemanding. And best of all, he *got* her. But he'd still be all of those things tomorrow, and she'd just have to wait.

Curse Valentine's Day, Victoria thought as she sat staring at the impotent phone in her hands. Then she had another thought: What she didn't like about the holiday was that it controlled people, dictated how they were to feel and act. If she didn't call him simply because it was Valentine's Day, then wasn't that just another way of letting the holiday control her? Of course it was. Besides, her feelings for Jason were something completely separate from the blasted day. She didn't love him because the calendar said to; she loved him because…holy shit! She loved him!

Victoria traced a fingertip across the text of Jason's message, and this revelation suddenly seemed like something she'd known for a long time, but now she was ready say it out loud.

"Oh God," she groaned, "not on Valentine's Day!" Now she definitely couldn't call him.

Unless, well, if he did come over, it probably wouldn't be too difficult for Victoria to persuade him to stay for a sleepover. She could keep her mouth shut until coffee the next morning, couldn't she? Sure she could. Without allowing an opportunity to talk herself out of it, she madly dialed his number. She chuckled as she dialed, because he'd probably known that she was going to break at some point and had just been biding his time, waiting for it to happen.

He picked up on the second ring. "Hey, baby."

Victoria felt the warmth of a blush flow into her cheeks at the sound of his voice. "Hi. What're you doing right now?"

"I'm out with the lads. We're going to catch the new *Torturer* movie in IMAX 3D."

"Oh. Isn't that, like, three hours long?" Her eyes flicked over to her clock, 8:25, and she felt the blush fade from her face.

"Yeah, about that. Look, we're pulling in now, so I'd better run."

"Yeah, sure. Bye," Victoria said as quickly as she could and hung up.

Why hadn't she left everything as it was? Why hadn't she just watched another show, done some reading, and gone to bed? No, she had to get herself all worked up over Jason, put herself out on a limb only to…to what? To find out that he'd carried on this Valentine's Day without her—like she'd asked him to? That he wasn't sitting at home just waiting for Princess Victoria to summon him?

Of course he wasn't sitting at home pining for her. Another of the qualities she could add to her list of things she loved about him was his independence. And her situation was not any different than it had been five minutes earlier, so why had this unwarranted feeling of dread crept into her gut? She tried to shake it off, but failed. That one phone call—one stupid phone call that she shouldn't have made—had thrown all of her assumptions out the window. She had assumed that Jason had gone along with this quarantine on Valentine's Day all for her benefit, but now she wondered if the real reason Jason had so readily agreed was because he didn't *want* to spend Valentine's Day with her; he'd rather be out watching cyborgs blow things up with the guys.

Victoria understood that this was quite a jump to make from the previous twenty-second conversation, but there was such a thing as women's intuition, and just then Victoria's intuition and three glasses of wine were telling her that she was in love with a guy who was nowhere near sharing her feelings. She considered that she should probably feel fortunate to have learned this before it was too late, like with Martin, but this time it didn't feel like she was better off knowing. This time it felt like she would've been happy living in oblivion for a little while longer. She got up and dumped out the last two inches of wine.

"Stupid Valentine's Day. Stupid, stupid Valentine's Day," she grumbled as she watched the red liquid swirl down the drain.

There would be no telling Jason that she loved him, not until she heard it coming from his mouth first, and who knew when that would happen, if ever. All Victoria wanted to do was to put yet another abysmal February 14 behind her, so even though it wasn't even nine o'clock yet, she changed into her jammies and climbed into bed. She read for a while, and then drifted off to sleep.

Victoria was jolted awake by an angry buzzing. She swung her arm over and slapped the snooze button on her alarm, but the racket didn't stop. She stared at the glowing red numbers and let them come into focus—12:01—before she realized that it was her door bell.

"What the hell?"

She rolled out of bed and picked her sweatshirt off the floor, pulling it on as she padded to the front door. Looking through the peephole, she saw Jason standing there wagging his eyebrows up and down at her.

"Such a dork," she laughed to herself as she turned the deadbolt. When she pulled the door all the way open, he was standing with a bouquet of mixed flowers held out in front of him.

"Happy February fifteenth!"

Victoria tilted her head slightly and pulled her eyebrows together. Was Jason really standing here with flowers?

"You didn't say anything about the day after." Jason smirked and stepped in to give Victoria a kiss on her wrinkled forehead.

"Jason…I…." She was still trying to fully wake up and get a grip on what was happening. Meanwhile, Jason's lips peppered her face with kisses, and he worked his way down to her mouth. Victoria threw her arms around his neck, parting her lips and letting herself melt into him. If this was a dream, it was one of the most delicious she'd ever had. Besides, there'd be no risk of saying that she loved him if her mouth was otherwise occupied.

Jason eventually pulled back, but continued to cup her face with his free hand while he brushed his thumb softly over her lips. She wanted to tell him so badly. She clamped her eyes shut and willed herself not to say it.

"Victoria…."

"Jason…."

"Baby, will you *please* spend next Valentine's Day with me?"

Victoria opened her eyes. It was time that she stopped blaming the holiday for her own insecurities and bad decisions of the past. If this man—this wonderful man—in front of her ever decided to tell her he loved her, what the hell did she care what day it was when he said it? And if it took him until next Valentine's Day, she would wait.   Her throat clenched with a rush of emotion, so she nodded her silent agreement. Jason's lips spread into a wide smile.

"One more thing," he added, as he brushed back the hair from her forehead with his fingertips. "I love you."

That's when Victoria started crying. And not just weeping; all out bawling. Her shoulders shook and she squeaked as she tried to say it to Jason, too. But it was going to be a while before anything coherent came out of her.   Victoria wasn't prone to emotional outbursts, but she suddenly felt like Scrooge on Christmas morning, like the Grinch with his heart busting the scales. The Valentine's curse had been broken, and Victoria was in love with someone who loved her just as much.

Better Than One Dead Rose and
a Monkey Card
Jessica McQuinn

Brady Jansen could feel a warm breath brush across the back of his neck, causing his body to come alive. Cracking one eye open, he looked at the glowing red numbers of the clock on the dresser. His heart raced when he saw that it was 7:24, which meant that he was going to be very late for work.

Panic and dread shot through him for a brief second before he realized it was Saturday…glorious, work free, lazy Saturday.

With that thought in mind, Brady rolled over to reach for his wife, only to find the big blue eyes and the syrup-sticky face of his four-year-old daughter, Ryann, where his wife should have been.

"Daddy's awake!" she yelled as she hopped off the bed and scurried out of the room.

"Damn!" he cursed quietly as he realized that, in fact, it wasn't a glorious, work-free, lazy Saturday. Instead, it would be a basketball, yard work, kid-filled Saturday…again. With a groan, Brady's arm flopped over his closed eyes and he thought back to when he and Whitney had first been married. He really loved his family, but there were days when he longed for the times before kids when he and Whitney could stay in bed and love each other all day long if they wanted, or he could take her in the middle of the kitchen floor, or the living room, or the backyard....

Remembering those early days had Brady's blood heating up once again. It was so hard anymore to get any time alone with his wife. Their lives were so busy that the only time they had together lately seemed to be when they were both sleeping.

As Brady lay in bed, fully awake after the cold reality of his life had hit him right in the face, he could hear the sounds of that life happening around him.

"Alex, go get ready for your game," he heard Whitney tell their nine-year-old.

"But Mooom...." The returning whine from his daughter was shrill and made Brady cringe as an image of his life in another four years, when she would be thirteen, flashed in front of his eyes. Wondering if he could get his own apartment for about ten years instead of living in a house full of hormonal women, he let out a small moan.

In that moment, it hit him that it was Valentine's Day, and that meant a "day of obligation." The way that he figured it, there were five days like this throughout the year: New Year's Eve, Valentine's Day, Father's Day, his birthday, and their anniversary. Before kids, Christmas was on the list too, but now they were so exhausted by the end of the day that all either of them cared about was sleeping.

Brady thought about his plans for the night, and knew that there was no way Whitney would be able to resist him, and he *would* get his wife naked in the bed, so there was a ray of hope.

He definitely wasn't looking forward to the day he had to survive before that dream could be made a reality. The only thing that was going to get him through it was the hope that Whitney would be so impressed with him at the end of the night that she would reward him by wearing some of those lacy, girly things that he could peel off.

"Daddy's awake! Daddy's awake!" Ryann's voice was loud, and the happiness in it made him smile.

Just then, the baby cried, and while Brady appreciated that Whitney had let him sleep in, he knew that his "me" time for the day was over. With a groan, he rolled to get out of bed. Pain almost brought him to his knees, and taking a gander down at his boxers, it was more than apparent that even through all the chaos going on around him, the idea of having Whitney this morning was still a driving force for his body. He thought that maybe he would be able to get a few minutes alone with her sometime during the day, just enough time to ease the want that currently was taking over his entire thought process. A man had to have goals….

Brady jumped in the shower, taking a few extra minutes to try and ease his body's demand before pulling on his gym shorts and a T-shirt. With a deep breath, he headed out into the craziness that was his life.

❧

"Whit! Do you know—" Brady was cut off as he turned into the kitchen and was confronted with his wife's shaking, exquisite, round bottom. She was still in her little pajama shorts and one of his old tank tops, her dark curls pulled back into a ponytail that was swaying along with her rear end. Standing at the sink, she was washing the pans from breakfast. Her earbuds were in and she was completely oblivious to her husband's presence.

Leaning back against the granite counter top, his arms folded over his chest and legs crossed at the ankles, Brady was going to enjoy the show she was putting on. He had seen a plate of heart-shaped pancakes on the table, but watching his wife was much more interesting than food at that point.

Even after ten years of marriage, Whitney could still make him hard just from looking at her. Brady adjusted himself carefully as he looked around for the kids. Fortunately, they were all in the family room, watching whatever cartoon was on. He turned back to his wife's perfect, supple ass still shaking to the music.

Whitney had a thing for 80's hairband music that Brady could never understand, but whenever she was in a good mood, the house was filled with anything from Warrant to Bon Jovi. He had spent several years teasing her about it, but in truth, she was damn sexy when she was dancing around the house to the shit.

Unable to take it any longer, he pushed himself off the counter and crept up behind her. As his arms encircled her waist, Whitney jumped a little, dropping the pan she'd been washing in the soapy water. Brady's hands moved up her sides, a sly smile playing on his lips as he realized she wasn't wearing a bra under the thin material of her shirt.

Whitney was surprised when Brady's arms came around her and slid up along her body. She loved when he touched her, but with three kids and jobs it was rare that he did it anymore. In fact, since the baby almost eight months ago, he'd only reached for her in bed a handful of times, so feeling his hands on her body made her sigh and lean back against him.

"Happy Valentine's Day, baby," Brady whispered in her ear before nipping the lobe.

"You remembered?" Whitney laughed as she turned into Brady's body, his strong arms holding her to him. There were bubbles on her cheek and the shirt she was wearing was almost see-through from the splashing dish water. She had never looked more beautiful to him.

"Of course. What, do you think that I'm that much of a Neanderthal that I would forget my girl today?"

"Well, you did last year…and the year before…and—"

"Okay, okay! I get it. I know that I suck at the romantic crap, but tonight, I will make up for all of the ones that I forgot."

"So I'm not getting one almost-dead rose and the card with the monkey on it from the gas station this year?" There was a small smile teasing the corner of her lips as Whitney looked up at her husband.

"Hey! I believe there were *three* almost-dead roses." Brady's voice was light and teasing in response to the look that his wife was giving him. "Tonight…." He leaned in to place a delicate kiss on Whitney's lips. "And if you could wear that little red dress? You know the one. Be ready at seven."

"Ummm, you did remember that we need a babysitter if you're planning to take me out, right?" Whitney wasn't going to get all excited, knowing that there was little chance that Brady would have thought that far ahead.

"Of course. I'm not a total moron. Shay will be here at six-thirty so she can get all the instructions and other crap before we leave." The smile on his face was nothing less than radiant, and Whitney leaned in to kiss him, a laugh bubbling up from inside as she did. The fact that he was so proud of himself was just too funny to her.

Needing more than that small peck, Brady pulled his wife closer to him as he captured her perfect pink lips with his own, enjoying the sweetness that was so familiar to him. There had never been anything better than kissing Whitney…well, there were things better, but at the moment he was more than happy to have her body against his and her mouth moving with his. Until….

"Ewww!" The girls had come into the kitchen, and the sound of their disgust was in stereo as they both said it at the same time.

Brady smiled against Whitney's lips as he placed one more small kiss there. Letting his arms drop from around her, Brady stepped back and scooped up Ryann in his arms.

"Daddy, why do you kiss Mommy?" Ryann asked, her eyes shining. She was the inquisitive one, which he loved.

All of his girls were so different, and if you looked at them, you would never know they were related. Alex was the spitting image of Brady, with straight, almost black hair that she kept short; dark, expressive eyes; and the build of the athlete that she was. Alex was the boy that he didn't have. She was the tomboy of the bunch, playing soccer, softball, basketball…name a sport and Alexandra not only loved to play it, but she excelled at it.

Ryann, on the other hand, was lighter than her sister, favoring Whitney's side more with light brown curls and deep blue eyes. She was smart as could be, and Brady worried about when she'd start using her brains for evil.

Of course he didn't know what Charlie would be like, but at eight months, she was already a bit of a princess. With two older sisters that treated her like their own personal baby doll, she really didn't stand a chance.

"I kiss Mommy because I think that she is beautiful and I love her," Brady told his daughter.

"So does that mean that Jason Montross loves Alex and thinks that she's beautiful?" The innocence in Ryann's voice was in total contrast to the sly smile that was on her face as she eyed her older sister. Brady knew she was getting closer to that line between good and evil.

"Ryann! You are such a tattletale!" Alex exploded and tried to leave the kitchen. She didn't get far.

"Hold it, young lady." Brady felt like he had just added ten years to his life hearing that his tomboy daughter, at nine years old, had been kissed.

"Brady," Whitney warned as she gave him a look that he knew meant if he said and did what he was thinking, which was that they were going to home-school Alex and keep her in her room until she was 30, then she would risk committing the sin of withholding her body from him on a day of obligation.

Alex looked up at her father, completely mortified that her sister had told everyone that Jason had kissed her. It wasn't like she had liked it; it was kind of gross and she'd told him not to do it again or she would punch him in the stomach, but she definitely didn't want her parents to know, and especially not her dad.

"Who is this Jason? I'm going to need to talk to him. Now that you are going to have to marry him." He winked at Whitney, who was a little wary of where her husband was going with this.

Alex went from mortified to sick to her stomach instantly.

"Wh-wh-what do you mean, Daddy? I'm not going to marry Jason."

"Yeah, Daddy. Alex said that they broke up and aren't going to get married anymore," Ryann added, to her sister's complete mortification.

Brady's head began to pound out a rhythm along with his heart that had quickened in pace. He had started out just to tease or even scare Alex, but hearing that his nine-year-old daughter had "broken up" with a boy had all of his "Dad Reflexes" kicking in.

"Oh, well, when a boy kisses you, it means that they have to come talk to me and then you have to get married. You don't see me kissing other girls or Mommy kissing other boys, do you? Because we're married." Brady was trying to keep a straight face, but had to bury his face in Ryann's hair so that Alex wouldn't see him.

Unable to speak, Alex swallowed hard. Tears were brimming in her eyes and Brady was feeling bad for torturing her, but he wanted that boy in front of him. No one needed to be kissing his daughter, let alone thinking they had some sort of relationship that they could "break up."

"I think that we should meet this boy, don't you, Mommy?" He looked at Whitney and hoped she would play along with him. She definitely wasn't happy with him, but nodded her head.

With a booming clap, Brady said, "Okay, so you go get ready for your game. Mommy can call and invite this Jason over for a nice Valentine's lunch. We'll all have a nice *family* meal." There was special emphasis on the word "family" just to make Alex panic a little more.

"Brady." Again there was a warning in her voice, but Brady wanted this to be a lesson not only to all the boys that she would ever know, but to all of his daughters as well.

"Go on, Alex. You have to be at the gym in twenty minutes."

"Daddy! I'm only nine! I can't get married," Alex cried out as she headed to her room to get ready for her basketball game. Her mind was racing, and the fact that the whole thing was all that stupid Jason Montross' fault seemed to be the one thing in the forefront. Just because they had been boyfriend and girlfriend last week didn't mean he could kiss her. Alex vowed that she was definitely going to punch him in the stomach as she slowly made her way to her room to change for her basketball game.

Once Alex had slammed the door of her room, Brady set Ryann down and kissed the top of her head. "Go check on Charlie, baby." Watching her run to the family room, he turned back to his wife. Instantly he thought he might be in trouble. Whitney was standing with her hands on her hips, tapping her foot like she was sending an SOS, and she was not smiling.

"Brady. That was so not the right way to handle this."

"You didn't say anything." He tried to look like he knew what he was doing, but in all honesty, his "Dad Reflexes" had simply taken over and the need to scare any and all boys away from his little girl had been the only thing that mattered.

"Yeah, because I don't want to make you look like the jackass that you were being in front of your daughters," Whitney shot back.

"Baby...." He began to walk out of the kitchen, heading to their room. Brady coached Alex's basketball team, and he needed to get his jersey and some shoes. Whitney followed right behind him, her voice almost a whisper so the kids wouldn't hear her.

"Don't you dare 'baby' me, Brady. Did you even look at Alexandra? She was horrified. And really, do you think that your gung-ho sports fanatic daughter was happy about a boy kissing her?"

By this time they had made it into the bedroom, and even though he was in trouble and starting to think that maybe his wife was right, the more important thing to him then was getting his hands on his wife.

Whitney had just stepped into the room when Brady caught her, and in one movement, he closed and locked the door as he pinned her body against it. His hands were holding her hips as he began to brush his lips along the column of her neck. For her part, Whitney still wanted to be angry, but having her husband's hands and lips on her and the feel of his body pressing against her had her distracted.

"Brady…." There was more that she wanted to say, but her mind and her mouth simply wouldn't work together any more. Everything in her body was screaming that she not only wanted the man who was making her vision blurry just from his touch, but she needed him.

"I know, you're right, Whit." Brady's words were soft, and the feel of his breath on her skin caused the flesh to burn for him. "And I'll let Alex off the hook. I promise. But let's do this…so I don't look like an ass in front of my girls." Slowly, the tip of his tongue grazed across her collarbone, and Whitney's knees went a little weak.

"Fine," she breathed out, not caring anymore that she was going to be aiding her husband in scaring the crap out of not just their daughter, but a poor unsuspecting boy. Her only concern was the way that her husband was touching her and how she could get him to do more.

"Daddy! We're going to be late!" Alex's voice pierced the little bubble that Brady and Whitney had created for those few minutes.

"Crap!" they both said at the same time before breaking into laughter. Brady leaned his forehead against his wife's and let out a sigh. Looking into his lust-filled eyes, Whitney thought of how lucky she was to have a man like Brady. Yeah, their life may not be perfect and *he* sure as hell wasn't, but he loved her and their family and was a good man. It didn't hurt that he was still as hot as the day she met him, either.

Unlocking and pulling open the door, he swatted Whitney on the ass and said, "I'll be out in a minute. I need to…ummm…yeah." He turned and walked into the closet to find his jersey.

A few minutes later, Brady came out of the bedroom to his daughter, who was now looking very much like her mother: dark eyes boring into him, hands on her hips, eyebrows pulled into a V. Once again, he felt that feeling of dread set into his chest for the future. He was going to have to scare a lot more boys as the years went on, that was for sure.

"All right, sport. Let's get going." He ignored his daughter's look and walked right past her into the garage.

Behind him, he heard her "Mooommm…."

"Talk to your dad, Al" was all that Whitney said to her daughter. She did feel bad, but Brady had already made such a big deal about it that there was no way they couldn't follow through. Of course, it was left to her to call the boy's parents (fortunately she was friends with Nicole Montross) and prepare a lunch that two nine-year-olds would like, not to mention cleaning the house before this all took place. Now that Brady wasn't scrambling her mind and trying to get her naked, she was thinking more clearly and she was getting a little pissed off.

Brady was already in his truck when Alex finally came out. The look on her face was so sad that for a minute he almost gave in and told her that they didn't need to have lunch with the boy and she wasn't going to marry him…or anyone if he had anything to say about it. But then he thought about Ryann and Charlie, and how eventually they would be in the same situation, and unfortunately Alex was going to have to be the sacrificial lamb in this case.

Hopping into the back of the extended cab, Alex buckled herself in and folded her arms over her chest, glaring at the back of her father's head.

"Cheer up, honey. It won't be so bad. It's important that I meet him. I mean, if you're going to marry him, I need to make sure that this guy can take care of you." Brady couldn't help teasing her a little more as he started the car and backed out of the driveway.

"Daddy!"

"Alex," he whined right back at her. "I'm sorry, but if you're going to go around kissing boys, then this is what we have to do. Do you think that I'm happy about marrying you off so soon? I mean, I hope this Jason kid has a job or gets a good allowance."

"I didn't kiss him, Daddy! He kissed me. I told him that if he kissed me again, I would punch him in the stomach."

The smile that spread over his face almost hurt. At least he knew that he was doing something right, except she *should* have punched the kid. Thinking back to when he was nine, he couldn't remember wanting to kiss girls. In fact, he distinctly remembered

Becky Hammerstein trying to kiss him and he ran to hide in the boys' bathroom. Brady really didn't like this Jason kid.

"That's my girl," he said under his breath, hoping she wouldn't hear him.

"I don't even like Jason anymore. Please, Daddy, I don't want to marry him. I want to be grown like Mommy and marry someone like you."

That was pretty much it for Brady. He didn't know if he was being played by his oldest daughter, but with that one statement, she melted his heart.

"Okay, maybe since you didn't kiss him, you don't have to marry him." He heard a breath release from Alex and felt bad about how worked up she had gotten over this. "But, I'm still gonna meet this kid and we are going to have lunch. I want him to know that he can't just kiss you." With a quick look in the rear-view mirror, he could see the look of relief on her face. "You know that, right? No boy ever has the right to kiss you or do anything else if you don't want them to…and you won't *ever* want them to."

"Daddy!" Alex rolled her eyes at him as he glimpsed at her in the mirror. That was all Brady needed to finally breathe for real since hearing about a half-hour ago that his baby girl had been kissed.

It was after eleven when Brady and Alex walked back into the house. As they came into the family room, Ryann was lying on the floor, and Charlie was in her play-seat watching a Disney movie that was playing on the DVD player. Two small heads swiveled to quickly look at them.

"Hey, baby. Where's Mommy?" he asked Ryann, who had turned back to whatever princess was singing in that nasal voice.

Without even looking at him, Ryann replied, "Mommy said a bad word and that she was going to take a shower."

Brady's body responded to the idea of Whitney's naked body under the stream of hot water as steam frosted the glass around her. He had no idea what had gotten into him. Never before had he wanted his wife the way he had since the moment he opened his eyes that morning. Even when they were first dating and she would send him home with only a blissful kiss and memories of the feel of her curves, he didn't crave her like he did right in that moment.

While Brady had never believed in the whole hype of Valentine's Day (thus the forgetting most of the time), it was the only thing that he could come up with as to why his body had been in a constant state of arousal. The *why* didn't really matter to him; all that did matter was getting into the bathroom and helping his wife with those hard to reach places.

"Alex, go get ready. Your friend will be here soon," he told his oldest daughter as he leaned down to kiss Ryann's curl-topped head.

"Daddy, Mommy said a *lot* of bad words. I think you should stay here with me and Charlie." Ryann pulled her attention away from the princess on the screen for a moment to look at him. Brady's love for his daughter grew immeasurably at her words. The fact that she wanted to protect him was one of those things that made him remember why he loved being a dad.

"I think I'll be okay, Ry. Mommy is a sucker for a cute face." Brady winked at her and went to give Charlie a kiss, his mind focused on the sound of water running and the images that was creating for him. Then it hit him: an odor that could revive the dead.

With a silent curse, he picked Charlie up. As much as he would have loved to just lock himself in the room with Whitney, there was no way he could do that to the beautiful little girl who was smiling and cooing at him. Not to mention if Whitney was already mad that he was late getting home, leaving this little surprise would definitely have him back in the days of a memory and his own hand at the end of the night.

"All right, princess. We've got company coming, and while I think that this stink bomb would make a great weapon." Ryann let out a squeal of laughter. "Your mom is already mad at Daddy, and we just can't have that, now, can we?"

Mussing Ryann's hair as he walked past her after picking up the baby, Brady headed to Charlie's room to get her nice and fresh, the minutes ticking away and taking his hope of shower time with Whitney with it.

Sure enough, by the time he'd finished changing Charlie, putting a new princess movie on for Ryann, and dealing with Alex's rant about the fact that Jason was actually coming to the house, Brady could no longer hear the shower.

Thinking that he could still catch Whitney before she got dressed and maybe have time for a little pre-big-event fun, he opened the door to the bedroom and slipped in. Ensuring the door was locked, lest any of the little people who wandered the house interrupt, Brady headed for the bathroom…and his wife.

When he saw her, he was completely struck speechless. Bent over in front of him in a pale pink lace bra and matching panties, Whitney was blow drying her hair. It was like a scene from a bad coming of age teen movie; everything seemed to be moving in slow motion, and for some reason, he could hear Whitesnake playing in the background.

Shaking his head to try to get blood flowing again, he realized that there was no blood left above his waist. Every male instinct in his body flared to life at seeing the woman he loved like that. Her skin still held the slight blush from the heat of the water, and as she straightened up, her dark hair fell in curls over her shoulders. Whitney was glorious. There was no other word that Brady could even pull to the front of his mind. She was just glorious.

"Oh my God!" Whitney screamed as she jumped at the sight of her husband's body framed in the open door. "Jesus, Brady. You scared me to death." Her heavy breathing from the scare was causing her breasts to rise, which in turn caused Brady's arousal to twitch.

"Sorry, baby. I was just completely hypnotized by you standing there looking sexier than I have seen you in a very long time."

"Right, because me blow-drying me hair is so erotic?" Whitney laughed.

"You have no idea." Brady let out on a breath as he pulled his shirt over his head.

"Ummm…you know you're going to get lucky tonight, right? You don't have to woo me here, Brady. I mean, if you got some after the dead rose and monkey card, there's not much you could do to blow it now."

Oh God! Did she have to say 'blow'? Brady thought as he slid his gym shorts and boxer briefs down, the mental images of his wife and that perfect mouth and what he wanted her to do with it playing in his head.

"Really? 'Cause Ry said that you said a *lot* of bad words while I was gone." Brady laughed as he reached out to Whitney, encircling her wrist with his fingers and pulling her to him.

"Yeah, I said 'damn' and 'crap' a few times. Where the hell were you? This lunch was your idea, you know."

"I'm sorry." He kissed her lightly. "I took the girls for some doughnuts after the game." Brady's hands glided over her lace-covered hips on his way up to cup both of her perfect breasts in his palms.

"Brady, this won't work. I'm not going to let you distract me," Whitney admonished as she slipped out of his grasp.

"Oh, come on, Whit. Look at me." Brady gestured to the impressive hardness jutting out toward her. "I need some help here. It will only take a few minutes. Please, baby." He poked his lip out in a pout, hoping that it would sway her slightly.

"Oh, my poor baby," Whitney cooed to him, running her hand over his bare chest and teasing her way down to where he was praying her hand would end up. Instead, she backed out of the bathroom. "Tell you what, you get in the shower and maybe get started a little without me, and I'll be right back to help you." She disappeared around the corner, and Brady let out a small moan at the thought of finally having her touch him today.

Brady stepped into the glass-enclosed shower, a huge smile almost splitting his face. He turned on the water to a perfect warm temperature and leaned his head back to allow the water to flow over him. With his eyes closed, he could almost imagine that it was Whitney's hand moving down his body instead of his own.

Ding Dong

The sound of the doorbell made Brady's eyes peel open. Standing on the other side of the shower door was his wife, fully dressed in jeans and a red long sleeve t-shirt. Disappointment wouldn't even be a strong enough word to describe what he was feeling.

"Aww, babe, don't look like that. I promised I would help you out."

The shower door opened, and Brady closed his eyes in anticipation of her hands on his body. There were no hands. Instead, he let out a small scream as ice cold water began pelting his body.

"There, that should help you." She laughed, and Brady heard the bedroom door close at the same time that the doorbell rang again.

"Whitney!" he screamed. Brady couldn't believe that Whitney had teased him like that. Now he knew where Ryann got that devious little mind of hers.

Given how his body had been betraying him for the entire day, Brady decided to leave the water ice cold. It didn't help matters, however. While his arousal was instantly doused by the cold water, his mind was still firmly focused on Whitney. Mentally, he counted down the hours until he could have her and let out a small groan at the realization that it was going to be too long.

Whitney couldn't help but laugh as she walked down the hall to the front door. Brady deserved that shot of cold water, and she didn't regret it at all. That was a little bit of karma for leaving her with all the work while he went and played with Alex and ate doughnuts. Another little laugh bubbled up as she thought of how his eyes shot open when that cold water hit him.

Opening the door, Whitney found Jason Montross. The poor kid had to know that this was not going to be a fun play date with Alex. He was already shaking as he stood on the doorstep.

"H-h-hi, Alex's mom," he stuttered out. Whitney had to push down the giggle that tried to escape at the sight before her. She only hoped that Brady would take it easy on Jason.

"Hi, Jason. Come on in. Alex is in the family room with her sisters. Go ahead and head in there. Lunch will be ready in a few minutes. I'm making peanut butter and jelly."

"Well, Jason. How are you doing, *son,*" Whitney heard Brady boom with a special emphasis on the word "son."

There was no reply from the boy.

Whitney didn't want to see the carnage so she went into the kitchen to make lunch instead of into the family room. From behind the bar, she could see her oldest daughter curled into one end of the couch, Jason cowering on the other end, and her husband right in the middle of them. Brady's big arm was stretched across the back of the sofa almost touching both kids.

The thought that Alex was only nine and that this was just the beginning hit Whitney as she gathered the ingredients for lunch.

Between all three girls, there were going to be lots of boys stuttering their way through meeting Brady, and she was going to have to be the voice of reason on all sides. She knew that no boy would ever be good enough for Brady to trust with any of his daughters. It was something that she both adored about him and dreaded having to deal with.

While she made the sandwiches, using a cookie cutter to cut them into heart shapes, bits and pieces of the conversation floated in to her. Brady's voice was light and teasing, so she knew he hadn't gone in for the kill yet, but was just playing with his prey.

"—stud, you are the man."

"—yes, sir."

"Daaadddy!"

"Lunch is ready!" Whitney called, hoping to save her daughter from dying of embarrassment and Jason from peeing his pants.

As they all sat around the table, it was quiet and awkward. Brady eyed the boy, but kept a smile on his face, while Whitney tried to ease some of the tension.

"So, Jason, do you play any sports? Alex had a basketball game this morning."

"Uhhh…yeah, I play soccer," he said without lifting his eyes from his plate.

Following his wife's lead, Brady jumped right in. "So, Jason, you go around kissing girls a lot, do you?"

Alex choked and coughed while Ryann giggled. Jason's head came up fast to look at Brady, his eyes open so wide, it looked like he was in a wind tunnel. The boy's jaw was moving like he wanted to say something, but the words weren't making it out of his mouth.

"Well, I'm just trying to make sure that when you and Alex are married, you won't be kissing Katie or Abby and breaking my little girl's heart. Because that would not make me happy…"

A small squeak from Alex threw Ryann over the edge, and she fell to the floor laughing and holding her belly.

"Ummm…uhhh…ummm…uhhh…." Jason was so worried about the fact that Brady was still completely focused on him while Ryann was rolling on the floor that he couldn't even get a single word out.

"Oh, and you have a job or get an allowance, right? Alex is a girl after all, and girls need lots of things that cost money." Brady continued to bombard the kid with information that he knew was scaring the shit out of him. Unlike with Alex, he didn't feel bad at all about it.

Jason still hadn't said a word and Brady still hadn't looked away from him. He could hear Whitney trying to get Ryann back up off the floor and into her seat, a task not made any easier by the fact that their daughter's antics had apparently been appreciated by her younger sister, and Charlie was squealing and giggling too.

"You see, I like to make sure that no one *ever* touches my girls if they don't want them to, and if I'm going to hand one of them over to you…I have to make sure that you are going to take care of her."

"Okay, Brady. That's enough." Whitney's voice was a little harsher than she had intended it to be, but the kid looked like he was about to cry, and Alex was red from head to toe from embarrassment.

"Uh-oh," Ryann piped in from her end of the table, where she was finally back in her seat. "Daddy's in trouble. Oh, Daddy, just look at Mommy and it will be okay. Remember, Mommy is a sucker for a cute face."

Brady knew that was not going to go over well. He also had a sneaking suspicion that his perfect, beautiful four-year-old was a devious little troublemaker. Looking over at Whitney, he could only shrug. Whitney just glared at him, thinking that she would make him pay for that comment later.

At Whitney's words, Jason had looked over at her. Pulling her death gaze from her husband to look at the small boy, she could actually see tears brimming in his eyes and was sure that Brady had done what he intended to do.

"Jason, Alex's dad, while not doing things very well, is a little concerned with you kissing her. We think that you both are too young to go around kissing. Do you understand?"

Jason looked over at Brady, who was locked on the kid like he was a Russian Mig and Brady was Tom Cruise in *Top Gun*. Taking a deep breath and mustering up all of his courage, Jason finally spoke. "I only kissed her because Kaleb Michaels dared me to. I don't want to kiss Alex.…" His words were cut off by Brady's lips pulling up into an actual snarl.

Brady had no idea why the little kisser saying that he didn't want to kiss his daughter bothered him, the whole damn point of this lunch was to make sure he didn't want to go within one hundred yards of Alex. But to hear a boy say that he didn't want to be near his daughter, well, that just pissed him off.

"I mean, I like Alex and all, we play soccer, and baseball, and basketball at recess. She's like, really fun, but girls are kind of weird and loud. I don't want to kiss any girls. But, Kaleb called me a chicken, and then said if I kissed Alex he would give me his SpongeBob DS game for a whole week." Jason hadn't taken a breath since he began talking and had to take several deep ones when he was finished.

"Ah, well, who can pass up SpongeBob?" Brady asked with only a hint of sarcasm that was completely lost on the nine-year-old.

"I know. It's the brand new one and my mom won't buy it for me. And since Alex is the only girl that I even like, I just kissed her."

Suddenly, Brady's face relaxed slightly when he realized that this was more about a video game than his daughter. That he could understand a little bit more. He thought that at nine, he probably would have braved kissing a girl for a video game, too.

"Here's the thing, Jason," Brady started, and the smile quickly faded from the little boy's face. "You can't just go around kissing girls without their permission. That's not nice, and I think you're pretty lucky that Alex didn't pop you one when you did it."

They all looked at Alex who put her head down quickly so no one could see her smile. She knew that her mom wouldn't like that she was thinking that she was still going to sock him one.

"And as you get older, you might have someone, like me for instance, who will have something to say about it. Got it?"

"Ye-ye-yes, sir." The boy was back to being scared out of his mind.

"Okay, eat up, and then I'll kick your butt on the Wii for a while." Brady smiled at Jason.

Swallowing hard, the boy eagerly dove into the rest of his sandwich. Whitney looked across the table at her husband, and her heart beat a little faster that he belonged to her. She loved that he was protecting his girls, but was kind enough to understand the boy a little bit.

There must really be something in the air today, Whitney thought, because just like he had been all over her, Whitney wanted Brady in a way that she hadn't experienced in a long time.

Lost for a minute in her thoughts, Whitney was pulled back to reality when Charlie began screaming. When she looked around, the table had cleared, and it was just her and her youngest daughter left.

"Well, it looks like you and I have been ditched for bowling or hockey or whatever they're playing, huh, baby girl?" Whitney took Charlie out of the high chair, deciding to change her before grabbing a book and curling up with her on the couch. She hoped Charlie would sleep and that she could get some reading done.

☙

"Whit? Hey, baby," Brady whispered while he gently shook his wife. It was almost three in the afternoon, and he had just sent the Jason kid home after a humiliating defeat in Wii Bowling. Whitney had fallen asleep with the baby on the couch while he had played with Jason and the girls.

Placing a light kiss on Whitney's forehead, he felt her stir under him.

"What time is it? Why did you let me sleep so long?" Whitney's sleep-heavy voice went right through Brady's body, settling in his groin and once again making him hard. It seemed that pretty much everything she did or said today had that effect on him. Hell, he knew just catching a whiff of her would cause him to go granite-hard today. It wasn't like she didn't get him going on every other day, but today there was something more. Brady thought that maybe it was because he had planned so well for later that he knew his reward would be extra special. If one dead rose and a monkey card got him laid, man, he could only imagine what Whitney would do for him tonight.

"First, it's about three o'clock, and second, because you obviously needed to sleep. I feel bad for throwing all this stuff at you today and wanted you to enjoy yourself and relax for a little while. Jason went home a little while ago. He isn't such a bad kid…as long as he keeps his lips away from my daughter, I'm good."

Brady's hands were running the length of Whitney's arms causing goose bumps to spring up along the path he was taking. Whitney thought that was odd, because it felt like her blood was heating up in her veins.

"You know, the girls are pretty occupied...." Brady touched his lips to his wife's. Whitney let out a sigh in return.

"Sorry, Brady, I've gotta run to the store for a few things. Damn! I can't believe I slept the afternoon away. I have to have something for Shay to eat tonight or she will never babysit again. I mean, do you know how hard it is to get a babysitter in this neighborhood? One of the reasons she will still come is because I always have Pepsi in the fridge and a pantry full of snacks. Not to mention that once the kids are down, she has free reign on the phone and the computer."

"Oh, come on, Whit. Just, like, ten minutes?" Brady moved to give her a more passionate kiss in hopes that it would get her worked up enough to agree to ten minutes locked in their bedroom. He never made it.

"Not gonna happen, big guy." Whitney pushed her husband off of her and got up from the couch. Patting Brady's cheek, she left him sitting alone as she went to freshen up before going to the store.

Brady went to check on the girls on his way to his office to make sure his plans for the evening were on track. The plan was that they were going to Whitney's favorite Chinese restaurant; then they were going to head over to a drive-in movie. He knew that it seemed cheesy, but when they were dating in college, they spent almost every summer night there with chairs in the back of his old beat up pickup truck. And even though it was summer, they would spend a lot of time under the cover of a blanket....

Of course, he had arranged for flowers to be at the restaurant, and the back of the truck was already packed for the movie. Brady knew that he was going to score big with this one.

"I'm going to the store. I'll be back," Whitney hollered from the kitchen and Brady heard the garage door a minute later.

❧

When Whitney finally returned home, it was almost five o'clock. It was amazing to her how busy the grocery store was on Valentine's afternoon. The majority of the people were men who wandered aimlessly with heart-shaped boxes tucked under their arms as they crowded the card aisle. The other shoppers seemed to be stocking up to cook that special dinner, so the pasta aisle was jam-packed as well.

Whitney had had Brady's gift tucked away for weeks. In reality, it was more for her, but she knew that he loved when she took the time to put on some nice lingerie, and the red satin bustier with the matching panties would be something that he would enjoy taking off her. She couldn't wait to see the look on his face when he saw her in it.

The house was quiet when Whitney walked in and that made her nervous.

"Hello?!" she called out.

"In here, Whit!" Brady's voice echoed down the hall.

After setting the bags of groceries on the kitchen counter, Whitney headed to see what everyone was doing. Usually, when things were quiet, it meant that she was going to have a lot of cleaning to do.

To her surprise, Whitney found Brady in the girls' bathroom with Ryann and Charlie in the tub. He was singing some silly made-up song as he washed Ryann's hair. The fact that she wasn't screaming bloody murder was a feat in and of itself, but to see her laughing made Whitney smile. Immediately her body began to heat up. There was nothing sexier than seeing the man she loved being a great dad to their girls.

"I ordered pizza for them for dinner," Brady told her as he glanced over his shoulder at her. Whitney could only wonder how long it had actually been since they'd been together, because Brady was working awfully hard to make sure that he got lucky later.

"Ummm…okay. I guess I'll put the groceries away, and once the pizza gets here, I'll go get ready?"

"Sounds good, babe." Brady turned back to the girls in the tub just in time to get a face full of bubbles. With Ryann and Charlie's giggling little voices behind her, Whitney went out to put the snacks she'd bought for the babysitter away, her smile bigger than it had been in a long time.

Once the pizza arrived, Whitney went to get ready for her big date. Brady had already gotten dressed and looked especially handsome in dark slacks and a blood-red dress shirt with the top few buttons open, giving a little preview of his incredible chest. She left Brady to make sure the kids ate and didn't make a mess. Really, it was like leaving the monkey in charge of the zoo.

A little while later, when Whitney walked out of the bedroom, Brady and the girls were in the family room playing Candy Land. Much to Whitney's surprise, the dining room table was cleaned off and the place looked perfect. She made a mental note to flirt with Brady more often if it made him work this hard to get her in bed at the end of the night.

As she walked into the room, every head turned to look at her. This made her a little nervous. It wasn't like she never dressed up, but the occasion was so rare that she fidgeted and tried to pull at the hem of her dress.

"Mommy, you are beautiful!" Ryann said with actual surprise in her voice. Whitney wasn't sure if she was pleased or insulted.

"Yeah, she is," Brady commented. "But Mommy always looks beautiful," he added as he looked her right in the eye. He could tell by the way that she was fidgeting that she was uncomfortable. although he couldn't imagine why she felt that way. She was still the most beautiful woman that he had ever seen; even after being together for over twelve years, there had never been another woman that he wanted.

"Jeez, Ry, you sound like Mommy never looks pretty. You are such a four-year-old," Alex scolded her younger sister. Whitney smiled at her, pleased that even though her father had embarrassed her to no end today, she had rebounded and was back to her usual bossy self. "You really do look pretty, Mommy," Alex added.

"Thank you, everyone. I think Daddy's looking pretty handsome, too." Whitney had barely finished the sentence when the phone rang.

Brady reached over to the end table and answered it. He didn't take his eyes off of his wife's amazing body as he spoke into the phone. "Hello?"

Whitney walked over and took Charlie out of his arms while he talked. He said "yes" and "really?" a lot, and Brady's face turned hard, his eyebrows pulled down low and his mouth set in a frown. This was never a good thing.

"Sh…" Brady started as he hung up the phone. A quick, wide-eyed look from Whitney had him swallowing the curse before it could fully escape.

"What's wrong?"

"That was Shay's mom. Shay is sick. She can't babysit tonight." Brady's voice was deflated. "Guess we're in for the night, babe. I'm sorry."

Whitney tried not to let the disappointment show on her face. She knew that Brady was feeling bad that their evening had been ruined and didn't want to make him feel worse. Not knowing what to say, she just stood there with the baby in her arms thinking that she might as well go change into her pajamas.

While he could hear the girls chattering, Brady wasn't listening to any words; he was thinking of what he could do to save the evening. He had wanted this for Whitney so badly. Yeah, he knew there would be benefits that he would reap, but everything he had done had been for her, because she deserved more than what he had done in the past.

"Okay! I have a plan," Brady suddenly announced. When Whitney looked up at him, she saw one eyebrow quirking up, making him look a little sinister. Judging by that expression, she wasn't sure that whatever idea he had come up with was going to be a good thing.

"Ummm…it's almost seven o'clock on Valentine's Day, Brady. It's not like you're going to find another babysitter. Hell, even my sister had a date tonight, and we both know that's saying something."

"No problem, Whit. Why don't you put Charlie to bed, and I'll be back in half an hour, hour tops." Brady was already pulling his cell phone out and was dialing as he headed out to the garage.

Whitney could only shake her head as she went to the kitchen to get the baby's bottle before putting her down for the night.

"Girls, I'll be in the back putting Charlie to bed. Try not to make a mess please," she called out to her daughters. The thoughts about what Brady could possibly be up to were running rampant in her mind, and all she could think was that it was going to be bad and cost a lot of money to fix. His "plans" usually did.

Brady was on the phone ordering dinner for the two of them before he even got in the truck. If they couldn't go out for the night that he had planned, then he was going to bring the night to her. As long as they could get the girls in bed when he got home, then things could actually still work out.

On the way to Mr. Chow's to pick up the food and the flowers he'd arranged to be there, he made one stop to complete his plan. Being a logistical thinker was always an asset when plans had to change and you had to improvise. This was nothing new for him.

About an hour later, Brady pulled back into the garage with all of his supplies. It was later than he had hoped, but that would work in his favor with getting the girls into bed, so he shrugged it off and focused on making Whitney happy—happy enough to finally let him get his hands (and other body parts) on her.

Brady found Whitney and the girls tangled together on the couch where she was reading to them. He was pleased to see that Whitney hadn't changed clothes and was still in that curve-hugging red dress. He loved her in that dress, and she didn't wear it nearly enough for his liking.

Unable to take his eyes off of everything that he loved, Brady stood in the opening between the kitchen and the family room just watching three of the most important women he would ever have in his life. Once Whitney finished the story she was reading, he planned to usher the girls off to bed and then the two of them would eat while the girls fell asleep.

Whitney caught her husband's eye and smiled up at him. She couldn't deny that she was disappointed that their first night out in almost a year had fallen apart, but she was still happy that she had what she did, and seeing the gorgeous man that she was lucky enough to call her own staring at her with so much love in his eyes seemed to be enough.

"The end," Whitney finished and closed the book. Both Ryann and Alex yawned. "I think that it's time for bed." Of course, even after the yawns, the girls argued with her, but she easily herded them down the hall to their rooms.

Brady followed behind them, going to tuck Alex in first while Whitney did the same for Ryann. As they passed each other in the hall, Brady took the opportunity to hook an arm around his wife's waist and pull her in to a deep passionate kiss.

"What was that for? Not that I'm complaining," Whitney asked on an exhale, her breath bathing Brady's skin in warmth and causing his entire body to harden for her…again.

"For the same reason as this morning. Because I think that you're beautiful and I love you," Brady said as her released her and walked into the room Ryann shared with Charlie.

After tucking Ryann in and kissing the sleeping baby, Brady went back out to the kitchen to get the food that he had left there. He put the bouquet of lilies in a vase and set them in the middle of the table with two candles.

A few moments later, Whitney came in and actually stopped dead in her tracks on seeing what Brady had done. Her hand flew to cover her mouth and tears stung the corners of her eyes. Brady had *never* been a romantic guy. When he proposed to her, it was on New Year's Eve, right in the middle of the first time that they had sex. The moment that she had dreamed of her entire life amounted to him panting out that he loved her and wanted her forever just before he finished. In truth, until later that night as they lay together, she didn't even know that it was his actual proposal. That part came as a total surprise.

So, to see the lit candles, her favorite Stargazer lilies, and plates piled with what smelled like Mr. Chow's was a huge thing for her husband. Seeing the look of surprise in Whitney's eyes and the tears that he could tell she was trying to hold back made Brady feel like an ass. The woman that he loved should never be moved to tears because he brought dinner home for her. It made him realize how much he had been neglecting *them*. Yeah, he took care of his family, worked a good job, paid for a nice house, scared the crap out of boys who got near one of the girls. But, he hadn't been taking care of *them*. That was going to change.

"Okay, so I wanted to take you to Mr. Chow's tonight, and these were going to be on the table." He gestured to the flowers. "But since I couldn't do that, I brought everything to you." Brady stood and walked to her chair, pulling it out for her to sit.

Dinner was nice, and they held hands, Brady stroking the back of her hand with his thumb while they ate. They talked about things other than the kids for a while, but eventually the conversation came back to them. This was their life, and they were both content with it, even if sometimes it wasn't convenient.

"Thank you, Brady. That was great. I haven't had Mr. Chow's in so long," Whitney said as she looked down at her empty plate before sitting back in her chair with a sigh. "This was such a good idea. I have to admit, I was a little worried when I saw that look in your eyes and you used the word 'plan.'"

"Oh, there is more to the night, so don't let your guard down yet," Brady said as he stood to clear the table. "You sit tight for a few minutes; I am going to get some things ready, and then I'll come and get you."

Whitney wasn't surprised when she watched him walk into the bedroom. She knew that the night was heading there, and honestly, she wanted him badly. What *did* surprise her was when he came back out a few minutes later and went into the garage. She could only watch him walk past her, a big smirk on his face and a twinkle in his eye, and then admire his rear-end and the fit of his slacks as she turned to watch him going out the door.

Sitting in the quiet house, Whitney let out a long sigh. It was rare that she had any time to enjoy the quiet. Usually, if there weren't kids running around, then the TV was on some sporting event or war movie. Whitney closed her eyes and thought about how good Brady looked in that blood-red shirt with his dark hair and eyes, and heat began to pool low in her belly. That's when she heard and smelled something that made her open her eyes and whip her head around to look in the kitchen.

The last thing that she had expected tonight was her husband to make popcorn. She wondered briefly if there was some new trick he was planning to use popcorn with in bed. Making a note to start checking the history on the computer and block any of the freak sites where he would have gotten this idea, Whitney tried not to imagine just what was going to be done with the popcorn.

Brady was standing in front of the microwave waiting for the popcorn to finish popping. He had set everything up out in the garage and this was the last thing that he needed. Part of his plan had been to go to a drive-in movie, and he was still going to try and do the next best thing.

When the microwave indicated that the popcorn was done, he poured it out into a big bowl, grabbed some sodas out of the fridge, and stopped next to his wife, who was still seated and staring at him. Her eyes were big and round, the blue of them almost swallowed up from the black of her pupils.

What the hell does she think I'm planning that has her so apprehensive, he thought before realizing she had sex on the brain, and he had popcorn in his hands. He let out a low chuckle.

"Come on, babe. I've got the rest of our date ready." He pulled the chair out with his foot as his arms were overflowing with popcorn and cans of soda.

"Ummm, honey? Where exactly are we going? Just because the kids are asleep doesn't mean we can leave." Whitney thought that maybe he had lost his mind. At least that's what she hoped. Because now she was worried about all those times that she had left Brady with the girls. Had he even stayed home, or did he just throw some Goldfish in the middle of the floor and let them fend for himself while he went out with his buddies?

"What? You think that I'm that much of an idiot? I have a surprise in the garage."

Whitney reluctantly followed her husband out the door. She couldn't begin to imagine what kind of Valentine's surprise he could have put together in a stinky, tool-filled garage. The dead rose and monkey card were looking pretty good at that moment, as she tried to think of one thing she would find romantic or sexy in their garage.

Brady held the door open with his body while Whitney walked past him. His eyes locked on the shape of her ass under the tight red material, and he was really happy that he had come up with this. In the end, he thought this was actually going to be better than the original plan, because this way, he could get his hands on his wife without having to worry about other cars around them.

"Climb on in, baby. In the back. I have everything ready."

Whitney did as she was told and opened the door to the back of the extended cab. Instead of booster seats or sports equipment that would normally be there, she found a pile of blankets and several boxes of movie theatre type candy. The movie screen was dropped and ready for use. Climbing up into the nest that Brady had created, Whitney hoped the movie would be something fun and romantic.

"So, what do you think?" Brady asked as he climbed in behind her. He had pushed the front seats as far up as they could go and then put them forward so that there was more room in the back.

The pride was more than evident on his face with the big smile he was sporting.

"This is great, Brady, but I don't like not being able to hear the kids." She felt bad that he had gone through so much trouble, but the thought that one of the girls could wake up and need her made her nervous.

"Thought of that, too." Brady smiled as he pointed at the baby monitor on the dashboard. Whitney had to give him credit; he really had thought of everything.

"Well, I have to say that I am impressed. What movie are we watching?" She waited, knowing that this would be the final thing that would determine if her husband had been kidnapped and replaced by a very life-like android, not sure if she would try to get the old Brady back if that was the case.

"Oh, that's the best part." He clicked the remote and the menu screen for *300* came up. Whitney let out a small groan, but at least she knew that the man she was about to let grope her in the back of the truck was really her husband. "See, I know that you like to look at that Gerard Butler guy. I get some good warrior fighting, and there is even a love story."

"Um, the wife being left at home and having to fight off other men is not a love story," she told him as he slid his arm around her and pulled her close. It really didn't matter what they were watching, and really she expected nothing less from Brady. The fact that he had gone through so much just for her was all that counted. She snuggled into the warm protective arms of the man she was lucky enough to be loved by.

The movie had only been on for about ten minutes when Brady began running his hands over the curves of Whitney's body. Gliding along the line of her hip, his fingers brushed the hem of her dress where it tickled her thigh. Seeming to have lost all control of her own body, Whitney slightly parted her legs in hopes that he would continue the journey.

Much to her delight, Brady did just that. Whitney's focus was so intent on what that hand was doing that she nearly jumped when his other hand skimmed over her breast. The sensation of having Brady finally touching her with no one to interrupt them had her lost and anticipating the moment when his fingers would finally find the part of her that ached for him.

"God, Whit…. I've wanted to touch you like this all day." Brady's breath was hot against Whitney's neck, and she shuddered as he lowered his lips to her neck at the exact same time his fingers reached the lace of her panties.

"Really? I never would have known." She tried to joke, but her voice was only a whisper and the sentence was punctuated with a gasp as Brady slid a finger under the elastic at the leg of her panties. He was teasing her, and she would let him…for now, because he had earned it with the evening he had put together for the two of them.

The movie was completely forgotten as Brady moved the hand under her dress to the top of her panties and began to slide them down over her thighs. "You won't be needing these." His voice was deep and dripping with want for her as his lips kept ghosting over the sensitive skin of her neck. The only response that Whitney could manage was a low moan on an exhale.

Brady had slipped his hand inside her dress, his thumb grazing over her lace-covered peak causing every nerve ending in her body to fire at the same time. Their love-making had always been good, but it had been a long time since it was great, and *this* was great.

Whitney felt like a teenager again as Brady's hand wandered back up the inside of her thigh, finally touching her where the heat was pooling in her body. She was slick with her desire for her husband, and the moan that escaped as he found the sensitive place where she needed him most filled the truck cab, drowning out the battle cry of the Spartans on the screen.

"Baby, I really want to do this properly, but I've wanted you all day, and I'm about to explode here. I need to feel you completely…be a part of you." Brady was dangling on the edge of ecstasy, and it showed in the tremble of his voice as he spoke. He didn't think that he would be able to hold on much longer and didn't want to embarrass himself like a high school kid with his first dirty magazine.

With a small groan, Whitney forced her body to move away from her husband. Scooting back slightly, Whitney moved her hands over Brady's body, unbuttoning each button of his shirt slowly, returning the torture that he had inflicted on her earlier as he played with her panties. Eventually, his expansive chest was exposed to her, and she leaned down to run her tongue along the dark trail that disappeared at his waistband. Her hands were still busy getting his belt undone and then his pants open. As her hand lightly passed over the impressive bulge covered by the thin cotton of his boxer briefs, Brady hissed between his teeth.

"Please, Whit…I'm going to explode. I need to feel you, baby," Brady choked out.

With a little giggle, Whitney tapped his hip to encourage him to lift his ass off the seat so she could get his pants off. Once he was rid of his stifling pants, all he could think about was that he was finally going to get what he had wanted all day: his beautiful wife loving him.

Carefully, Whitney moved so that she was straddling him, her dress scrunching up at her hips. The two of them sighed in tandem as she lowered herself onto Brady's waiting length.

"God, Whitney. I love you," Brady whispered as he held her hips still, adjusting to the feel of finally having her wrapped around him. He knew if she moved right then, it would all be over. When he had calmed down enough that he thought he could actually handle movement, he lifted up on Whitney's hips.

It took only a few minutes before Whitney found her own rhythm, and Brady moved his hands up along her sides and pulled her dress open, allowing him access to her perfect breasts. Capturing one hardened peak between his lips through the lace that covered it, his tongue teased her while his thumb roughly rolled over the other.

The movie played on, the sounds of battle combining with those of their love making as Brady watched his wife ride him into the most euphoric orgasm he had ever experienced. If he could have formed a coherent thought in that moment, he would have made a note that "super romantic guy" sex was a million times better than "one dead rose and a monkey card" sex.

"Brady…." Whitney gasped. Brady felt her body begin to tremble as her walls constricted around him, driving him to his own release. The sensation was so incredible that Brady wanted to be deeper within her body, causing him to surge forward so Whitney's body was trapped between him and the seat that was pushed forward as he continued to pump inside of her.

The blast of the horn as the headrest pounded against the steering wheel over and over echoed in the garage. While Brady knew it was happening, he couldn't stop his movements as Whitney panted under him. They both were so caught up in each other that they didn't really care about the noise.

When he was finally replete and Whitney had quieted, only a tiny moan still spilling out from time to time, her hands moving under his opened shirt over his back, he looked down at her. The lipstick that had been so perfectly applied earlier was smeared, her hair, which had been precisely curled and styled, was knotted and tangled. She was the most beautiful woman he had ever laid eyes on.

"Oh my God," Whitney breathed out at the same moment the baby monitor lights flashed and both Charlie's and Ryann's crying could be heard.

They looked at each other and laughed. Brady knew that he had woken them up with the horn, and he couldn't be upset that once again real life had crept into their time. This was their life, and as hard as things got some days, the fact that they were in it together was the best thing in the world.

"Well, considering I'm a bit more presentable, I'll go," Whitney sighed as she bent over and found her discarded panties, slipping them on before hopping out of the truck. "Why don't you clean up out here, and meet me in the room. I still have to give you your Valentine's present."

Brady groaned, daring to hope that unwrapping his present would result in his wife being naked. He watched Whitney disappear through the door, drinking in every perfect detail about her before starting to put himself back together and clean up the mess that they had made in his truck.

When he finally made it to the bedroom, he could hear the water running in the sink in the bathroom, so he knew that Whitney must have been able to get the girls settled pretty quickly. As he set the baby monitor back on the dresser, he saw—in the middle of the bed— one almost dead rose and a card. Brady didn't have to open it to know what would be on it.

He laughed out loud, but quickly stopped when the bathroom door opened to reveal Whitney in a red satin top and matching panties.

"Happy Valentine's Day," she said as she moved towards him. When she was close enough, he reached out and pulled her into his body.

"God, I love you, Whitney."

"And I love you. You know I don't need all of this. I love you because you are such a good man and a great dad, even if you make mistakes." She smiled up at him, and he lowered his lips to meet hers. "But, now that I know what you are capable of...."

Whitney pulled out of Brady's arms to crawl on the bed where she pushed up to her knees. The sight of her in that satiny thing in the middle of the bed ready for him made Brady sway a little on his feet as all the blood rushed to fuel his arousal.

"If you ever give me a dead rose and a monkey card for Valentine's Day, you won't get near me until Christmas." She laughed as Brady launched himself at her, pinning her beneath him as the evidence of his desire for her pressed against her stomach.

Leaning down to her ear, he whispered, "Not to worry, baby. But, I don't know if I've learned my lesson well enough. You might need to teach me some more."

"Oh, you must learn by repetition. This could take all night," Whitney replied as she moved her hips against him, causing Brady to groan.

"Daddy! Daddy!" The monitor that was back on the dresser lit up as Ryann's scared little voice rang out in their room.

Brady dropped his head to Whitney's shoulder and let out a long sigh.

"Daddy! Daddy!"

"Go on," Whitney said. "I'll still be here when you get back, and we have all night. Go take care of our daughter. Fight off whatever monster is hiding under her bed." She gave him a gentle push.

As Brady rolled out of bed, the same pain from the morning hit him and he sucked in a breath. This time, however, he knew that he wasn't going to have to wait hours for relief, only as long as it took to take care of the monsters in the closet.

As Whitney watched her husband's retreating form, she couldn't help but think that even with everything that had gone wrong in their day, it had still been better than one dead rose and a monkey card.

Home to Jackson
Victoria Michaels

Savannah London had pulled into her parents' driveway just after three o'clock in the morning. Her plane from New York had been delayed because of snow, then her connection into Memphis had to be de-iced, so it was no surprise that by the time her plane touched down in Mississippi it was well after midnight. Luckily for Savannah, the rental car company was open twenty-four hours a day. With her suitcase in the trunk and a large cup of coffee in her hand, she began the hour drive to her hometown.

Home. It had been nearly a year since she set foot in the house she grew up in. Even when she was away at college, she had managed to get home more often, but now, her career came first. It was one of the small sacrifices she made to keep her life moving according to her well thought out plan. As she sped down the highway, she couldn't stop herself from rolling down the window and breathing in the rich night air that told her she was almost home.

After her hellacious evening and long drive, all Savannah wanted was to crawl into bed, bury herself beneath the thick covers, and sleep until noon. However, bright and early the next morning, the very unwelcome sounds of a hammer and loud music began. Her eyes peeked open and looked at the clock, her fury building. She sat up in bed, and then screamed as a man with a scruffy beard crawled up a ladder outside her window, giving her a cheeky wink on his way to the roof.

"Mother!" Savannah yelled, pulling on her robe and throwing open her bedroom door. She stormed down the stairs like she had done countless times in her youth and tore into the kitchen, her socks sliding across the hardwood floor. "What kind of barbaric animals start ripping apart a roof this early in the morning?"

Her mother slowly turned from the stove, a tray of fresh biscuits in her hand. "Good morning, sunshine. Hungry?" Motioning her to the table, Savannah's mother set a plate out and held the tray as her daughter angrily snatched two biscuits and plopped them onto her plate.

"No, I'm exhausted. What's with the marching band up on the roof?" There was no butter in sight so Savannah went over to the refrigerator and stuck her head inside, looking for the yellow tub. "Do you know some strange man looked in my window? What if I was naked?" As she slammed the refrigerator door shut, there was a deep chuckle of laughter behind her.

"I'd say he was one lucky son of a gun."

Savannah's entire body seized up at the sound of his voice; not a single muscle would cooperate. Her head was screaming at her body to run or hide, knowing she must look ghastly having jumped right out of bed. But instead, her traitorous feet turned her around so she could lay eyes on the one man who, for years, had made her heart race and palms sweat—Jackson Whittaker. And based on the way her heart was trying to leap from her chest, he still had quite an effect on her.

His brown hair was long and wavy as ever, falling into his eyes and just past his shirt collar in the back. His cheeks were dusted with a few days' growth of beard that ran along his chiseled jaw line, and his blue eyes were just as bright and sexy as she remembered them. His tall, muscular body towered over hers, his chest and broad shoulders which were hidden behind a worn T-shirt begged to be touched. Perfection in a pair of jeans—that was Jackson.

Savannah and Jackson had known each other since they were children. From the moment the two met, sparks flew. They were like oil and water, their parents would always say; that was the only explanation for the explosive nature of their relationship. But the older they got, the more Savannah began to understand her strong feelings toward Jackson. She liked him—a lot. So much so that it infuriated her almost as much as he did.

They were opposites. Everyone loved Jackson, while Savannah was always "difficult" to get along with, her mouth often the main source of her troubles. In school, he had friends left and right while Savannah kept more to herself, often misunderstood by the other girls because she spoke her mind.

As children, Jackson did annoy her to the point that she wanted to strangle him, but in high school, things started to change. He would walk into a room, and instead of wanting to strangle him, Savannah's heart would beat faster…until he smiled at another girl. Then she'd want his head on a platter. Jealousy hit her like a ton of bricks, and soon she found herself using her sharp tongue and quick wit to keep him on edge and hide what she really felt for him.

As she looked at him across the kitchen, it was as if no time had passed.

"What the hell are you doing here?" The words came out much harsher than she intended, and any other man would have been offended, but not Jackson. He was as confident as ever. With an arrogant, dimpled grin, he leaned back against the counter and grabbed a biscuit, tearing off a piece and popping it into his mouth.

"Savannah Jane, I did not raise you to speak like that to a guest in our home, let alone Jackson. Did you know he came over here first thing this morning to help fix the leak in the roof before it ruined the ceiling in the parlor? He's nearly family. Now apologize."

Heat poured into her cheeks as they flamed with embarrassment at her mother's reprimand in front of him. Savannah nodded her head in Jackson's direction and whispered a nearly inaudible "Sorry."

Knowing her far too well and not one to let her off the hook that easily, Jackson pushed off the counter and followed her to the table, politely holding out a chair for her. When she was safely seated, he leaned over her shoulder. "I'm sorry, what was that? I couldn't hear you."

Savannah fumed at his teasing while her mother stifled a laugh. When her daughter's mouth fell open indignantly, Savannah's mother busied herself by the sink and waited for the fireworks to begin.

"I said I was sorry, but now I'm rethinking that statement."

He gave her hair a little tousle as he slid into the seat beside her and poured himself a cup of coffee. "Still grumpy as a rattlesnake in the morning, aren't you, Vannah?"

Savannah hid behind her long blond hair and bit the inside of her cheek to keep from smiling when he used the nickname he made up for her when they were kids. It had been a long time since she'd been called that, and every time she heard it, her thoughts immediately drifted to Jackson. Instead of answering, she found herself playing with the delicate necklace that hung around her neck as a distraction.

Life in New York was amazing, busy and bustling as all law firms were in Manhattan. She loved the city; she loved her job and was thriving at it. For the first time, she felt like she was finally moving in the right direction with her life. To her family, she was a huge success. A self-made woman. Savannah had finished college with honors a semester early and, without hesitation, bravely left the security of the small town she grew up in and headed off alone into the big city and made an incredible life for herself. To them, she had it all.

The move had been a very deliberate and planned choice. After college, she felt herself smothering at home in the small town, and it was getting more and more difficult to be around Jackson, seeing him with other girls and knowing the only thing they would ever have between them was a little chemistry and a lot of verbal sparring.

Desperate for a change, Savannah spent weeks researching law firms in New York so she could find the one with the best chance for advancement and promotion in the shortest amount of time. Tired of waiting for life to happen to her, she was finally taking charge. The moment she stepped out of the grimy taxi and looked up at the huge skyscrapers that lined the streets of Manhattan, Savannah knew she had made the right decision. This was where she belonged. This was where she could make all her dreams come true.

Assuming Savannah's silence meant victory in their battle of wills, Jackson winked at her, looking immensely proud of himself. Savannah, however, wasn't amused and laid into him again. "I'm much more pleasant when Peeping Toms aren't lurking outside my window first thing in the morning," she growled, taking another bite of biscuit.

"José."

"Excuse me?"

"Well, technically he was a Peeping José. That's his name."

Furious, Savannah threw a piece of biscuit at Jackson's head, earning her a stern glare from her mother. "His name is irrelevant; it's his actions this morning that are in question."

"*Behave*," her mother mouthed as she snatched a plate off the table and took it over to the sink before excusing herself from the room, snickering.

As soon as her mother was out of earshot, Jackson leaned in and whispered, "The lawyer in you still likes to win every argument, doesn't she, Vannah?"

"And you're still as infuriating as ever." She could feel his heated stare watching her every move, but instead of reacting, Savannah calmly focused her attention on her plate, counting the crumbs rather than daring to give him the satisfaction of seeing that he had once again gotten under her skin. Adding to her sour mood was the fact that whenever he was that close and looked that good, no matter how angry she was, all she could think about was kissing him. It had been that way for years, and it still drove her crazy. The man was sex on legs and he knew it. His favorite pastime was getting Savannah riled up, and for some inexplicable reason, she found that strangely endearing.

"I don't know why you two don't just kiss and get it over with. Jeez!" Savannah's older sister Marcy boomed as she appeared in the doorway, shaking her head as the two glared across the table at one another. While Savannah gaped at her audacity, her sister grabbed a glass out of the cabinet and poured some juice.

"Good morning, Marcy. You look beautiful today," Jackson said in a polite voice in an effort to annoy Savannah.

"Don't you try to play me, Jackson Whittaker. You forget who used to change your diapers." Marcy kissed her baby sister on the head and whispered, "I'm serious. Get the man in bed already. You two have been dancing around each other for years."

Savannah rolled her eyes dramatically, and even though she refused to admit it out loud, she knew her sister was right. She and Jackson had this unspoken "thing" between them. Usually they spent their time arguing, but then there were the quiet moments in between their squabbling, like now, when he would simply smile and look at her like she was the only woman on earth. Savannah couldn't help but be drawn to Jackson and wonder what life would be like…with him.

"How's the baby?"

A proud smile spread across Marcy's face. "She's an angel. Just like her mother."

"No, like her Aunt Savannah."

Both her sister and Jackson erupted in laughter.

Annoyed, Savannah went to the sink and tossed her plate into the soapy water. "And to think, I was going to offer to babysit for you tonight so you and Andy could go out to dinner, but if I'm such a devil…." She didn't even get to finish her tirade before Marcy came running across the kitchen and hugged her.

"You'd do that? Mom and Dad have that dance at the country club so I figured we'd be stuck at home tonight. Are you sure?"

Savannah winked at her sister then tugged on one of her many blond curls. "First, tell Jackson what an angel I am."

"Savannah's heaven sent—but you knew that already, didn't you, Jackson?" This time, it was his turn to blush, and the pink in his cheeks didn't escape Savannah's notice. "I have to go tell Andy he gets to take me on a date. We'll bring Jennie by around seven, if that's okay?"

Marcy finished her juice then flew out of the house, leaving Savannah and Jackson alone in the kitchen. When he stood up from his seat and came over to the sink, the room suddenly felt tiny. For some reason, whenever she was around him, she lost all her bravado and that exasperated her immensely. Jackson was so close she could feel the heat coming off his broad chest and smell the spicy scent of his cologne that enveloped her. Savannah suddenly remembered her tiny robe was hanging open and all she was wearing were the cami and shorts that she had slept in last night.

"That was really nice of you, Vannah." The deep, rich tone of his voice rumbled in her ears and sent a shiver down her spine. He reached out and brushed a stray hair back behind her ear.

"Yeah, well, don't tell anybody; I have a reputation as an evil, bloodsucking lawyer to protect." She tried to resist him but finally gave in and looked up into his eyes. She couldn't help but be amazed every time her eyes were met by the distinctively vibrant shade of blue... exactly like hers. Sometimes, when she looked at him, she swore she was looking into a mirror. A tiny part of her feared that because they had the same uniquely colored eyes, perhaps somehow he could see into her soul and know her innermost thoughts, or how she felt about him.

"Your secret's safe with me."

They stood for the longest time, inches apart—nearly touching, but not quite. His eyes kept dipping down to her lips, sending her heart into overdrive as Savannah's stomach started doing tiny flips in anticipation of what might come next. She hated that she reacted this way around him. She could question the most vile criminals on the stand without batting an eyelash, but this man could make her tremble like a little girl with just one look. She slowly ran her tongue across her bottom lip, making his eyes darken as he watched the trail of moisture shine temptingly, inches away. Jackson's lips parted and just as his head dipped toward hers….

"Savannah, baby!"

"Hi, Daddy," Savannah sighed, knowing the moment was ruined when Jackson nearly jumped across the kitchen at the sound of her father's voice. She tugged her robe closed and tried to look casual.

Her father looked back and forth between the two of them and grinned. "Am I interrupting something?"

"No, sir," Jackson said with a respectful tip of his head. "I was just getting ready to crawl up on that roof and see what José is up to."

Savannah's father grabbed his car keys off the counter and slapped Jackson on the back. "Thanks again, son, for coming over here. I know your construction company keeps you busy. You're always so kind to us." He turned to his daughter with a grin. "Savannah, we're running to the grocery. Oh, and your mother wanted me to remind you to, um, be nice." He held up his hands defensively and backed out of the room when his daughter's eyes narrowed with fury. "Don't shoot the messenger.

When he was out of earshot, Savannah exploded. "Has everyone around here lost their minds?" Jackson's deep laughter only irritated her more.

She stormed over to him and poked him square in the chest. "I'm going upstairs to take a shower now. Please try and keep your crew away from my window."

He grabbed her wrist, and before she could pull away, he brought her hand to his mouth and nipped at her fingertip. "I promise. As a matter of fact, I'll personally guard it for you." Instead of making her feel safer, the sly smile on his face made her heart race faster in her chest.

Trying to keep up her stoic facade, she stepped away and took one last parting shot. "If I see you outside my window on that ladder, Jackson, I swear I'm pushing you into the bushes."

"If you're naked or in a towel, it will totally be worth it." His rich, masculine laughter followed her up the stairs and didn't disappear until she slammed the door shut and fell back against it, gently hitting her head against the hard wood.

"Don't go there, Savannah, not gonna happen. You're here for three days and you have an amazing life in New York. This isn't part of the plan," she reminded herself as she headed to the bathroom and turned on the shower.

The rest of the day went by in a flash. Savannah spent the afternoon helping her mother bake ten dozen cookies for the dance her parents were going to later that evening. Jackson poked his head in when he smelled the first batch come out of the oven. With a mischievous wink, he grabbed a handful for himself and José then disappeared back up to the roof without even a word to Savannah.

Later in the afternoon, Savannah noticed the hammering had stopped and the house was suddenly silent. Determined to catch Jackson once more before he left, she quickly plotted a way to get his attention and put him in his place, once and for all.

"Mom, I'll go grab the mail." Savannah slipped on her shoes and headed for the front door.

As if reading her daughter's mind, Savannah's mother poked her head around the corner. "Jackson's already gone, baby. He and José left about twenty minutes ago. I heard him telling José he had plans tonight that he needed to get ready for."

"Oh." Savannah's stomach felt like it was full of lead. Of course he had things to do tonight. He was sexy and gorgeous. What woman wouldn't give her right arm for an evening with a man like Jackson?

Dejected, Savannah turned and instead of heading outside, she started to climb the stairs to her room.

"You okay, baby?"

"Who me? Yeah, Mom, I'm fine."

"Savannah, do you…."

She didn't let her mother finish her question; hearing her say the words out loud would make it all too real. "It doesn't matter, Mom. I'm only home for a few days, then back to New York."

"But I thought you said a while back you were considering leaving New York. We could use a brilliant attorney in town, you know."

Savannah shook her head, her long blond hair scattering into her eyes to hide the frustrated tears. "I'm not sure about anything right now. I have a great life in New York. I do miss…everyone, though." She waved her hand through the air. "I need to change. Marcy will be here to drop off Jennie in a bit."

After a good cry up in her room, Savannah dressed and then stared at her reflection in the mirror. She was smart and successful, yet she probably had been in love with Jackson since she was sixteen years old but had been too stupid to do anything about it. She had considered it, more than once, but in the end she never thought it was a viable option. Tired of mooning over everything she could never have with Jackson, Savannah set out on her own and made a life for herself—a life that she was incredibly proud of—all on her own. She went to college and then on to New York, but he'd never really left her heart.

It was back in high school, when a guidance counselor jokingly suggested she become a lawyer, that everything changed for Savannah. Suddenly, she found a place where her stubborn streak was valued and not considered an undesirable personality trait. Her determination and overly analytical mind were assets and had helped her land the job in New York, a job she was determined to be successful at—and she was. All the pieces of her master plan were falling perfectly into place, just like she had anticipated. And if she focused on that plan night and day, her thoughts never strayed…to him.

As she looked in the mirror at her sad, blue eyes, she realized that all her elaborate planning and stubborn streak might have cost her the one thing she never realized she treasured the most.

She ran her hands through her thick hair and allowed her fingers to dance over the beautifully polished stone she always wore around her neck. Convinced that somehow the small piece of jewelry was her good luck charm, Savannah closed her eyes and made a desperate wish on it, wishing for better things to come. She gave her reflection a quick smile and headed downstairs when she heard a knock at the door.

Outside, she found Marcy standing on the porch with a perfectly bundled Jennie in her arms. "Look, it's Auntie Savannah."

Jennie was as beautiful as ever. She was blessed with her mother's gorgeous curls and her father's bright red hair. Looking more like an angel than the last time she saw her, the baby reached her arms out to Savannah and flashed a smile that melted her aunt's heart.

"Hey there, baby girl," Savannah cooed as Jennie looked up at her with big blue eyes. "We're gonna have so much fun tonight—as long as you don't throw up on me."

"She's past that phase, Savannah," Andy said with a sigh as he followed his wife in the door, kissed his sister-in-law on the cheek, and dropped three bags onto the floor at her feet. "Just a few essentials for the baby, according to your sister. Thanks for doing this, by the way."

Savannah waved her hand in the air. "My pleasure. Mom and Dad just left a few minutes ago for the club, so I'm happy to have the company."

Marcy ran through her laundry list of instructions, showing Savannah how to mix a bottle, how to shake it up and test the temperature, and finally, she demonstrated exactly how Jennie liked to be held when she ate. When her sister offered to demonstrate how to change a diaper, Savannah shooed her and her husband out the door, wishing them a good evening.

The door closed and she kissed the top of Jennie's head as the infant tugged at her shiny necklace. "Looks like it's just you and me, kid."

No sooner had she taken three steps away from the door than there was a sharp rap on the glass behind her.

"Your mommy is a nut," Savannah whispered to Jennie. With a groan, she reached for the doorknob. "Marcy, I swear, I was just kidding about breast feeding her. It was a joke—" The words died in the back of her throat when the door swung open and she came face to face with none other than Jackson Whittaker.

He stood in the doorway looking like a dream. He was in a pair of jeans and a black collared shirt that clung to his chest like a second skin. His muscles rippled underneath the fabric as he ran a hand through his hair, nervously scratching the back of his neck. In his arms, he held a bag of food, a bouquet of flowers, and a bottle of wine.

"Jackson?"

"Hey, Vannah. Can I come in?"

"It's a free country." She stepped aside and allowed him to pass, slowly closing the door behind him. "Did you forget something?"

Jackson waved to Jennie and earned himself a happy squeal, then looked at Savannah in confusion. "No. Why would you ask that?"

"Well, it is Valentine's Day and Mom said you couldn't stop telling José about some hot date you had lined up," Savannah snapped as she tried to get Jennie to stop yanking on her necklace. Carefully she attempted to pry her niece's chubby fingers from the delicate chain, but Jennie wasn't letting go. Seeing her predicament, Jackson dropped what he was carrying and rushed to her rescue.

"Come here, princess. Now, we all want to strangle Auntie Vannah from time to time, but she seems to like that necklace, so let's give her a break." He chuckled and carefully lifted the baby from her arms and tossed her up on his shoulders, allowing Jennie to dig her busy hands into his hair and give it a tug instead.

Still unsure exactly why he was still standing in her parents' living room, Savannah scanned the items on the floor. "Flowers, food, and wine? Some woman's going to be very happy to find you on her doorstep." With tremendous effort, she faked a smile and silently wondered if she could get away with strapping Jennie in the baby carrier and following him to see who the little trollop was.

"You think so?" He grinned, not even trying to hide his excitement. "I was hoping she'd like all of this."

"Only thing missing is dessert…unless you have a chocolate cake in that back pocket of yours." Savannah pulled Jennie off his shoulders so he could gather up his things and leave. "You don't want to keep *her* waiting," she growled through her gritted teeth, imagining some other woman with her arms wrapped around Jackson's neck.

He picked up the bouquet of flowers and ran his fingers tenderly over the soft petals. "Well, I happen to know the girl I want to spend the evening with spent this afternoon making some damn tasty cookies with her mother, and I was kinda banking on her still having a few hidden in the kitchen."

Savannah looked at him blankly, blinking repeatedly as she tried to follow what he was saying. "Wait…what?"

He cupped her cheek and unexpectedly brushed his lips against hers. "I did all of this for you, Vannah. Would you be my Valentine?"

"Me?" She lamely wandered into the living room and plopped Jennie into the little activity center Andy had lugged into the house. When she felt Jackson's strong arm wrap around her waist she turned to face him.

"Yeah, you. Ever since your mom mentioned you were coming home, I've been trying to think of ways to get invited over here. I even considered cutting a wire or two and blacking the place out so I could run some new electrical while you were home." He ran his fingers over her cheek in a gentle caress. "Then the roof thing happened and it was like it was a sign from God."

"What changed? Why now?" Savannah was still reeling, unable to believe any of this was actually happening.

It was Jackson's turn to look embarrassed, his cheeks turning red as he glanced over her shoulder, afraid to meet her gaze. "I saw pictures of you and…the stiff."

"Excuse me?"

"The guy in the picture. Mister Armani Tux." Savannah watched the muscles in his jaw clench as he forced out the words. He nodded his head toward her mother's mantle. Off to the right was a framed picture of her and her long gone ex-boyfriend at a dinner party.

"Harry?"

Jackson shrugged. "I never caught his name. 'The Stiff' just seemed to fit."

Savannah swatted his arm and tried not to laugh. "I'll have you know he wasn't stiff at all."

"*That* doesn't surprise me either…."

She should have been shocked or offended at his comment, but all she could do when she saw the grin on his face was laugh. His deep, rich tones mixed with her higher ones, making the most beautiful sound.

"He was a nice man."

"If he was so nice, why did you two break up?"

It was a legitimate question, one Savannah wasn't sure exactly how to answer. Finally, she took his hand and held it against her chest, right over her heart. "Because he never made my heart do this…." Under Jackson's strong, calloused hands, Savannah's heart fluttered wildly like a hummingbird's wings.

The corners of his lips curved up in a slow mischievous smile. "Good. He better not have touched you either."

"I'm not a nun, Jackson."

"Thank God for that." He leaned over and pressed his forehead against hers, breathing in her perfume.

Savannah relished the tingling sensation as the pads of his fingers swept down the side of her neck before lacing themselves in her long hair. "Lemme get this straight. The reason you asked me out after all this time was because a *year* ago I had boyfriend?"

Jackson gave her hair a playful tug. "I didn't like it. Sue me." Savannah's eyebrow arched in an unspoken challenge, which he laughed off. "For a million and one other reasons that had nothing to do with the stiff and everything to do with my stupidity, I decided to finally man up and ask you out after all these years."

"Well, for the record, you didn't exactly ask me out. You showed up on my doorstep."

"You always have to be right, don't you?"

Savannah's chin dropped, her eyes glued to the floor. "I know it's annoying and drives everyone crazy. Sorry." *You aren't in a courtroom right now, Savannah,* she chided herself.

Jackson caught her chin and raised her eyes to meet his. "Don't ever be sorry with me. It does drive me crazy the way you argue—just not how you think." His arms tightened around her waist, holding her firmly against his chest. "I think the way you argue is sexy as hell, Vannah. Especially when it's with me."

Savannah's heart soared at his words, and without any warning or consideration of the consequences, she stood up on her toes and pressed her lips to his. Jackson lifted her up and off the ground, holding her in place and kissing her back with a fire she had only dreamed of until then. He tasted like mint and spice, and Savannah quickly discovered she couldn't get enough of this man. He lived up to all her fantasies and then some. Her arms clasped around his neck, her tongue seeking contact with his, a moan escaping from both of them at the first stroke.

In the blink of an eye, he had her up against the wall, his body grinding against hers as he continued ravaging her with his kisses. Savannah thought she would surely die from the pleasure of it all. Either that, or she'd wake up and find out it was all a cruel dream, one that she would never get out of her head. When she felt his teeth sink into her lower lip, Savannah let out a squeal of delight—and so did Jennie.

"Oh my God!" Savannah shoved Jackson off of her, sending him crashing into the couch before landing on the ground with a thud. "The baby."

Jackson picked himself up off the floor and laughed as he brushed off his pants. "Baby's fine, Vannah."

"But we were making out in front of her. She's too young to see that. I might as well have let her watch soft-core porn!" Savannah scooped the baby up and cradled her in her arms, feelings of guilt washing over her. "Marcy trusted me with her—"

"Fine. Let's get Jennie fed and to bed then, because I most definitely want to kiss you again." He shamelessly tugged at the collar of her shirt, allowing his fingers to dip down and examine the necklace that hung just between her breasts.

"It's beautiful," Jackson admired.

"It was a gift," she mumbled as she mixed up some cereal and a bottle for Jennie.

Jackson's eyebrow arched in curiosity. "From another one of your boyfriends?"

Savannah snorted, making Jennie laugh. "No. If I had a boyfriend right now I wouldn't have let you kiss me."

"Yes you would have," he said in a husky voice, his eyes locking on hers possessively.

Savannah nearly fanned herself to relieve the slow burn she felt building in her body. "Fine, but I would have decked you afterwards."

Jackson laughed and held up a spoon of cereal to Jennie's awaiting mouth. "That's my girl." Savannah spun around, not sure if he was talking to her or the baby. "When you get bigger and need dating advice, you better have Aunt Vannah on speed dial."

Faster than Savannah would have ever imagined possible, Jackson had Jennie fed and was cleaning up the mess....

"You in a hurry or something?" Savannah coyly asked from the kitchen as she sat on the counter, watching him.

"Yes. But truthfully, she's tired. Look at the way she's rubbing her eyes."

Savannah smiled at his astute observation. "How do you know so much about babies?"

As they carried Jennie down the hall for her bath, Jackson shrugged. "I hang out with Andy a lot."

He tried to escape her questioning, but Savannah's interrogation was far from over. She followed him into the bathroom and watched him fill the sink, checking the water temperature multiple times before lowering Jennie into the basin for her bath.

"And Andy always has Jennie with him when you two 'hang out'?"

"She's like a dog with a bone," Jackson whispered to Jennie loud enough for Savannah to hear. "Yep, when we play poker, she's sittin' on his knee."

Savannah held her tongue and gently lathered the shampoo into her niece's hair. She was acutely aware of how close Jackson was and the lustful way he was looking at her. When Jennie made an unhappy squeal, Jackson sprung into action.

"Can you grab the yellow duck out of the diaper bag? She always plays with it in the bathtub." When Savannah didn't move and stood there openly gaping at him, he rolled his eyes. "Your brother-in-law works a lot, but he likes to take Marcy out once a week...so I help out with the babysitting."

His explanation did nothing to bring her out of her stupor. If anything, she was even more stunned than a moment ago. Without taking her eyes off him, she blindly reached into the bag and grabbed the curved plastic duck. "Here, baby girl, it's your duckie."

Savannah held out the bright object for the toddler, and Jennie squealed as she held it tightly in her chubby hands as Jackson poured the water gently over her head. Instead of crying, she laughed.

Silently, Savannah watched him lather the rest of Jennie and then rinse her off. She was most impressed when he hoisted the slippery baby into the air and wrapped her up in a towel without hesitation. The way he talked to her, the way she responded to the sound of his voice, melted Savannah's heart. Here was this strong, powerful man cooing to the baby in his arms like no one else was in the room. There was no posturing or bravado on his part; he was simply acting on instinct with Jennie. He literally took Savannah's breath away.

"You really babysit her?" The words slipped from Savannah's lips in awe.

He handed her niece over and smiled as Savannah buried her nose in Jennie's hair, taking in the clean baby scent. "Yes, every Thursday we have a date, don't we Jen?"

"Why?" Together they made their way into the kitchen to prepare a bottle for the yawning girl.

"I love Marcy; she's a terrific mom. And Andy is my friend, so I wanted to help them out." He buried his hands in his pockets and shrugged. "I guess, in a way, I did it to be closer to you."

"You amaze me."

With a waggle of his eyebrows he grinned. "You ain't seen nothin' yet, Vannah."

She laughed out loud at his outrageous comment and took her niece to the couch to feed her the bottle. Much to her surprise, Jackson snuggled up beside her, wrapping his arm around her as she fed Jennie. "Look, you're a natural," he whispered as Jennie's eyelids began to droop in exhaustion.

Ten minutes later, Jennie was out cold and Savannah couldn't stop her hands from trembling as she laid the baby into the crib. Her kiss with Jackson had been amazing, but was it real or was it just shameless flirting on his part? And what did it mean after all this time? With a million questions rolling around in her head, she made her way back to the couch, clutching her necklace, running the stone back and forth across the chain nervously.

"Careful, you're gonna break that necklace, and it seems to be pretty special to you." Jackson patted the couch beside him, a devilish grin on his face that promised more kissing if she came within arm's reach. Wanting to buy some more time to figure things out in her head, Savannah sat on the arm of the couch, far away from his grasp.

"It is special. I've had it almost a year now, I guess."

"You never said who gave it to you." Jackson inched closer to her, his fingers nearly touching her thigh.

"That's because I don't know. It just showed up on my doorstep one day." She tried to scoot away, but Jackson was faster and caught her knee, his thumb gently massaging behind her kneecap.

"Accepting gifts from strangers? Is that a New York thing?"

"No." Savannah's hand went protectively to the necklace, covering the stone. Jackson's lips curled into a smile as he watched. "Fine, here's what happened. Last year, I came home from work and the necklace was sitting on my doorstep with no card, no note, no hint of who it was from. At first I thought it must have been a mistake, but when I called the store it was from, the woman assured me there was no confusion. She even laughed, saying the person who bought it had said I would call."

"It's a beautiful color," Jackson said as he reached out and rolled the stone between his fingers.

"I know," Savannah whispered, an embarrassing blush sweeping across her face. "That's one of the main reasons I kept it."

"The color?" Jackson's head tipped to the side as he studied her expression, trying to figure out what was running through her head.

"It—this is going to sound silly, but…it's the exact color of your eyes." She leaned down and ran her fingers over his cheek, tracing his high arching eyebrow before she kissed his closed eyelid. "Told you it was silly, but it reminded me of you, so I kept it." She shrugged her shoulders unapologetically.

"There's nothing silly about that." He laced his fingers with hers and grinned. "That's exactly why I bought it for you. The turquoise made me think of your eyes the second I saw it."

"The second *you* saw it?" Savannah nearly fell off the arm of the couch in shock. "Why didn't you tell me?"

"That is was from me?" Her head bobbed up and down. "I have no idea. Honesty, I was in New York on a long lay-over and too chicken shit to call you. But when I saw that necklace, I had to buy it for you. Then, when I saw you were wearing it in every picture your mom took during her visit this summer, I have to admit, it made my day to see you wearing it." His fingers wound their way tightly into her long hair. "Of course the pictures didn't do it justice. Seeing it on you now, I can't tell you what it does to me, Vannah."

Savannah slid off the arm of the couch and landed in his lap. Without hesitation she kissed him, her tongue teasing its way into his awaiting mouth and meeting his. There was nothing cautious or tentative about this kiss; it was full of fire and passion, just how Savannah wanted it to be. A cocky grin spread across her face when she saw Jackson's chest heaving as he gasped for breath—all from her kiss.

"Thank you."

"Honey, if that's how you're gonna thank me, I'll buy you a necklace every damn day."

She could see it all just within reach. The life she wanted with the man she longed for, a life full of fun and laughter…and children, just like Jennie. But then reality crashed down around her. This wasn't her life; she hadn't planned for any of this to happen. She was supposed to have a nice weekend at home and then head back to New York, back to the life she had built and loved. There was no way she was going to give that up on a whim, no matter how badly her heart was begging her to. She sadly shook her head and sighed, tears filing her eyes.

"My job is in New York."

He slid her closer, his chest brushing against hers as he cradled her in his lap. "You could always come home and practice here. Jackson isn't as flashy as New York, but it has its advantages." His finger swept a stray tear away as it fell.

Home…to Jackson.

"I don't know, Jackson. My life isn't here anymore. "

"But it could be, if you took a chance…on me. On us."

Savannah tried to get up and clear her head, but Jackson held firm, keeping her right where he wanted her. His lips strayed to her neck and began to kiss a trail up to her ear. "You aren't going to make this easy on me, are you?'

"No way. I've been a damn fool for waiting this long to let you know how I feel about you, Vannah. I've wanted you for years but have been too damn afraid to tell you."

"Really?" Savannah's breath left her in a rush, still unable to believe her ears.

"I want you…hell, cards on the table? I think I love you, Savannah. Always have, always will. By the time I worked up the nerve to ask you out, you were leaving for college and then for New York. It always seemed like the wrong time or you were on the verge of a new adventure in your life, and I wasn't going to hold you back. But now, every time I try and go out on a date, all I can think about is you and how the woman across the table from me isn't you. That or I stay up nights wondering where you are and who you're with and it drives me crazy." He made lazy circles on her thighs with his finger. "I love your wild spirit, your smart mouth, the way you don't take crap from me—or anyone for that matter. I want a life with you, Savannah. If you'll have me."

Savannah sat silently as Jackson poured his heart out to her, sharing his most intimate secrets. Part of her went into shock, unable to believe he had felt the same thing she had for so long and kept quiet about it. Nothing about the man in front of her was insecure; he was the picture of confidence. But he confessed that when it came to her, he was afraid…of her. The admission shocked her.

Her fingers instinctively reached for the beautifully polished turquoise that hung around her neck, hoping it would magically calm her. The necklace took on a whole new meaning to her now that she knew who it was from and what it meant to him as well. He cared about her…he wanted her. And he had for a long time. The only question was, would she finally take the plunge and be willing to go for something she truly wanted—not to prove anything to anyone else, but because she wanted it more than she wanted to eat or breathe? Could she and would she deviate from her well laid plans? Or would her head once again prevail over her heart?

She spent what seemed like hours looking into his eyes, searching for an answer about what she should do. Life in New York was amazing. But if she was being honest, there was still something missing, something that kept her up and restless in the wee hours of the morning. It was then that she realized what was missing: love. Yet somehow, in the arms of this man, the person she spent most of her life bickering with, she felt a peace she had never known. Even with all her success and achievements, nothing compared to this.

Head be damned, she whispered to herself as she reached out and cradled his face. Her fingers felt the light bristle of his beard, and

Savannah savored the erotic roughness of it. "I want a life with you, Jackson. You're the man I dream of at night, the man who I compare everyone to, but they all fall short. It's you, it's always been you."

His eyes filled with joy and desire, darkening with intensity. "You sure?"

"I've never been more sure of anything. I know there are a lot of things that we need to figure out, but you're everything I want, Jackson Whittaker. I love you." The words fell from her in a whisper as his hands roamed over her body, possessively exploring and claiming what was now his.

"I love you too, Vannah." His lips crashed into hers, the intensity of the kiss a searing heat that Savannah would have happily died from. He dominated her, willing her spirited body to follow his lead. Surprisingly, she allowed him to set the pace of the kiss, his tongue directing hers in how to move. He wasn't worried about scaring her with the knowledge of how much he wanted her; he saw it as proving his love. When Savannah was nearly breathless, he finally pulled away and whispered, "Forever."

Savannah grinned and confidently whispered back against his lips. "Forever…and always."

The Bridge
Alison Oburia

Kate Bennett leaned against the cold metal railing, watching the waves splash gently against the shores of the Ohio River. Five years had passed since the last time she'd stood here. Theoretically, she was in two places at once, standing on the bridge between West Virginia and Ohio right where the state line was marked, the sweet small towns of Williamstown and Marietta on either side of her.

She looked down at the worn card in her hands and read it again.

Do what you need to do, Kate. I'm going to give you five years to figure things out. If at that point you want to try this relationship thing again, meet me on the bridge on Valentine's Day, and we'll see where we are in our lives. I hope you find what you're looking for, but know that I'll still be right here. I love you. Dylan.

A tear escaped and she quickly swiped it away. Kate hadn't been ready for all that Dylan wanted: marriage, family, settling down in Marietta like his parents had. Her marketing degree was meant to lead her to big places, to do big things. She needed to see the world, make her mark in it before, as she'd put it to him, "being tied down for the rest of my life."

He'd loved her enough to let her go.

He'd never tried to contact her, nor she him, during all the time she was gone. As she stood on the bridge now, she knew she was a bit foolish to think that he'd even remember writing the note. Maybe he wouldn't show up, or maybe he'd walk up from Marietta with a wife and three kids. Didn't matter. She'd promised she'd be here on Valentine's Day, and here she was, alone and waiting for God only knew what.

Paul Workman tried not to let his emotions get the best of him again. Why was it that even a year later he still couldn't come here and not just lose it? He rested his hand on the larger of the two grave markers. Ginny's. He brushed the lawn clippings off the smaller grave, little Carlie's. They'd been his world. They'd grown up in Williamstown, he and Ginny. They'd married when they were fresh out of high school and went to college together. Seven years had passed before Carlie arrived, perfect and pink and healthy. By then they'd saved enough money so that Ginny could quit her teaching job to stay home to raise their daughter. Paul had become the high school's principal, so his income supported the family of three comfortably.

When Paul got the phone call from Ginny's sister to meet her at the hospital in Parkersburg, he'd shot out of the school and driven faster than he'd ever dared before. By the time he arrived in the emergency room, though, little Carlie, barely three years old, was gone and Ginny was on life support. The police met with him, providing details of the accident, but the words were garbled in Paul's brain. Large truck. Bad brakes. A red light that wasn't seen in time.

Two weeks after the accident, Paul, with his family by his side, gave the doctors the okay to let Ginny join their daughter.

He'd loved her enough to let her go.

Over the past year, he'd contemplated suicide a number of times, but he knew deep down that his family and Ginny's had been devastated enough. He couldn't do that to them. Paul wasn't healing, though.

"You're like a drone, Paul," one of the teachers had told him recently. "We all loved Ginny. But you've got to move on, man. You've got to find a way to let her go, allow yourself the opportunity to maybe find someone new."

If anyone had said this six months ago, Paul would have let 'em have it. Now, though, he was taking some steps to change things. He'd realized that going home to that empty house day after day was carrying him deeper and deeper into a depression that he didn't want to be in. His brother had helped him sell the place, Carlie's backyard swing set and all, and he'd moved into a small condo on the Marietta side of the river. He could still walk to work, but this move had provided the distance he needed from the pretty little two-story home he and Ginny had purchased a few years after getting married. He didn't want to keep running into his neighbors, their faces turning solemn every time they saw him.

This move across the river had also meant that Paul was truly on his own now, starting over. But was he ready to think about finding someone new? He grappled with keeping Ginny in his heart while he considered the possibility of making room to love someone else.

Too soon, he'd always say. Too soon. Maybe tomorrow or next month or next year.

⸙

The chill in the air had a bite to it, and Kate closed her wool coat around herself more tightly. It was nearing half past two; she and Dylan used to always meet between two and three. A few people had walked past, bundled and shivering as the wind whipped across the bridge. It was a great place to get in a good walk. The sidewalk was wide enough for people to travel side by side and, on warmer days, she imagined plenty of mothers with strollers would get their exercise crossing the bridge from one town to the other and back.

She could have been one of those women had she chosen to marry Dylan. His love was that little bicycle shop he'd bought, and he was content with staying right where he'd grown up. Every time she'd thought about living in such a small town, knowing there was so much more out there to discover, she'd gotten frustrated. She'd had big wings she needed to test out; the small cage called Marietta would have stifled her, broken her spirit. Kate sighed as she gripped the railing. "No regrets," she whispered. "You did what you had to, kiddo."

But Dylan had never left her heart or her mind. She missed him terribly the first few months she'd lived in Chicago, nearly broke down and called him many times that first year. Being on her own had gotten easier, as work kept her busy and friends kept her entertained. Looking back now, though, she could clearly see the superficial life she'd been living. As much as she'd needed to experience the fast pace and high fashion of the marketing world, the small-town girl in her still longed for home. A week back in Marietta would do her good.

The condo Paul had moved into less than a month ago had been cleared out hastily and haphazardly. The quick sale had helped him, but it also meant he took the place "as-is," leftover mess and all. What he knew of the previous tenant from a neighbor was sketchy: single guy, died suddenly of some kind of heart problem over Christmas break. God, he could feel the devastation the family must be going through, losing someone without warning....

As he'd cleared out some of the trash left behind, he'd put what looked like important papers in a box for the family. He found a few photos in a drawer of a couple, probably high school age, and they reminded him of how he and Ginny had been. Young and in love. In one picture, the boy was kissing the girl on the cheek as she looked into the camera with a smile. Turning it over, he realized he'd miscalculated their ages as he read the inscription: "Dylan and Kate, June 2004, Marietta College Graduation Day!"

Dylan. This was the man who had lived in the condo—the man who had died. He'd been about twenty-eight then, Paul guessed. He looked again at the woman, her gently waving auburn hair framing her face. She had beautiful green eyes, just like Ginny'd had. And the deepest dimples he'd ever seen. No wonder this man Dylan had kept the photo; from this and the other one where they'd leaned in to each other, smiling brightly, Paul could tell Dylan had loved Kate. With one more long look at the two photos, Paul placed them gently in the box with Dylan's other belongings.

More cleaning had resulted in Paul finding a set of letters and newspaper clippings in an open manila envelope. Given where he'd found them, in the corner of a shelf in the master bedroom closet, Paul figured Dylan had deliberately tucked them away a long time ago. As he began to read, he slumped down the wall of the closet, tears filling his eyes.

These were love letters never sent. In the first one, dated November of 2004, Dylan had poured his heart out to Kate, asking her to marry him, promising he'd do all he could to make her happy and help her reach her goals, pleading with her to stay, telling her he'd wait for her for as long she needed him to. The five other letters were all dated February 14, one for each year since she'd left. In them, Dylan wrote about how his business was doing and gave updates on his family and the town.

But he also filled the pages with how proud he was of her and all that she was accomplishing. Paper-clipped to each letter were articles and advertisements he'd cut out. He mentioned the marketing firm Findlay-Patterson, where Kate worked, and as the years had gone by he'd been keeping track of her promotions. The end of each letter, though, told the true story—that he wished she knew how much he missed her and wanted her to come back to him.

He'd loved her desperately, but she'd left him anyway.

The man had lived alone, and the few papers Paul had uncovered were in Dylan McCoy's name only. Kate had left and never come back. Paul was heartbroken for Dylan and sad that Kate probably never realized how much she'd hurt Dylan by leaving. He wondered if she even knew that he'd died.

It was when he was cleaning out behind the refrigerator the next day that he'd discovered that the story of Dylan and Kate hadn't ended with those love letters. As he'd pushed the appliance back into its place at the end of the long kitchen, a small, square note had been dislodged from underneath it.

Feb. 14, 2010—Meet Kate at the bridge at 3!!

The scribbled writing on the paper had been slightly faded and dust-covered, but certainly didn't date back to five years earlier when the couple had been photographed together. Given the exclamation points on it, Paul had guessed it had been written within the past year, as if Dylan had been counting down to the day he'd get to see his beloved Kate again on Valentine's Day.

ℰↄ

Kate hadn't kept in touch with too many people after she'd left Marietta. Her parents were in a retirement community in Cincinnati now, and her brother lived in Atlanta with his family. She'd booked a room at a small bed and breakfast for the week and chosen not to call anyone she knew in town. If Dylan didn't show up at the bridge, she didn't want others to know that she'd come back to meet him there.

She'd thought a little about what she'd do if Dylan arrived with someone—a girlfriend or wife. Surely she'd be polite and smile. On her drive from Chicago, Kate had concocted a story of being in a relationship with a VP of a big-name investment firm. He'd be a cross between Patrick Dempsey and Hugh Jackman, and they'd be planning to get engaged soon. She'd make up a story about accidentally forgetting to bring a picture of the two of them together, but she'd go on and on about how happy she was. She'd have to pretend all this to hide her broken heart.

It was nearing 2:45 and still no sign of Dylan. Kate decided she'd wait another thirty minutes, give him time in case he was coming from the bicycle shop or his parents' house or something. As another strong breeze hit her, she crossed her arms and shivered. Her glances toward Marietta continued as the minutes ticked by.

ℰↄ

Paul glanced up from the Sunday paper and over to the wall calendar his sister had given him. Today was Valentine's Day. He'd taped Dylan's note to the fridge when he'd found it a week earlier and still hadn't decided what to do about it. He wondered if this woman Kate had also written the date down and was planning to be on the bridge today, or if Dylan had been setting himself up for disappointment.

Maybe she wouldn't be there because she'd chosen not to come; maybe she'd forgotten about it.

Then again, maybe she would be there. But if she was, that would mean she hadn't heard that Dylan had died. Maybe she'd be standing there in the chilly weather, wondering why he'd not shown up. She'd never know that he'd planned to be there—had wanted to be there.

Not my concern, Paul had told himself every time he'd looked at that note on his fridge and allowed his thoughts to wander down the road of "what if."

After another look at the note, his eyes wandered over to the clock on the stove. It was getting close to three o'clock.

"Damn it," he growled as he grabbed his keys, the note, and his jacket and headed out the door to the bridge.

"Well, it's three o'clock, kiddo," Kate said quietly to herself. She sighed as she envisioned Dylan with a perky blonde, side by side at a playground, pushing their adorable children on toddler swings. Valentine's Day for them was being spent as a family. She'd known all along, since planning the trip a month earlier, that there was a good chance he wouldn't be there. That was the risk she'd taken when she'd left five years ago. As her eyes began to water, she gritted her teeth and reminded herself of the credo she'd adopted upon moving to Chicago. "No regrets."

But there were regrets. It was amazing the twenty-twenty hindsight one could have when realizing the path chosen may not have been the best one after all. Kate wouldn't wallow in self-pity, though. She'd wait the fifteen minutes she promised and then head back to the inn. Maybe she could check out with a minimal cancellation fee. It was Valentine's Day; surely others would like reservations at such a romantic place.

She allowed herself another glance to her right, toward Marietta, just in case. A man in a tan jacket, hands in his pockets, was heading up the walkway, but it wasn't Dylan. Once again, Kate turned to look over the water, her shoulders dropping in disappointment.

When the man stopped about five feet from her, she looked over at him quickly. He was now leaning his lower arms on the railing, his hands clasped in front of him, his jaw clenched. This man was in deep thought, Kate surmised.

Another few minutes passed in silence as the two of them looked out across the water. The sun was making the waves sparkle, and as Kate tilted her face upward and closed her eyes, she focused on letting the rays warm her.

"It's a beautiful day, isn't it?" The man's words surprised Kate. She opened her eyes and turned toward him, taken aback at his sudden comment.

"Yes. Yes, it is."

"I don't come here as often as I should. It's really very relaxing," he continued.

Kate stayed quiet, not sure why he was starting this conversation with her.

After another minute of silence, he spoke again. "You were going to meet someone here today, weren't you?" This was his second question to her, but again it was more of a statement, like he'd been expecting her to be here.

"Um, why do you ask?"

"Because you look cold, like you've been here a while. Like you've been waiting for someone."

Kate looked down at her hands, embarrassed. "Well, I'd sort of made a promise a long time ago that I'd meet a friend here today." She shrugged her shoulders. "He must have forgotten." She stood back from the railing, stretched her arms, and then tucked her hands into the pockets of her coat. "You're right, I am cold. I guess I'll be heading back inside." She gave him a smile and began to walk behind him, back toward Marietta.

Paul cursed himself internally as she began to walk away. *She doesn't know, damn it. Tell her.*

"Are you Kate?"

The woman stopped in her tracks and turned around, her head tilted in confusion. "I'm sorry. What?"

Paul couldn't look at her yet, couldn't face those green eyes that he knew would remind him of Ginny. "Are you Kate?"

"Yes…," she stammered. "How do you know my name?"

Paul turned to her as he pulled out the yellowed note from his pocket and silently handed it to her.

She accepted the paper hesitantly, but it was clear to Paul that she recognized the writing and saw her name on it.

"Where did you get this? Where's Dylan?"

Paul wasn't sure what he was seeing in the green eyes that pierced him now—anger, confusion, distrust, or a combination of all three. He inhaled deeply before speaking, trying to form in his mind the right words to say.

"I found that note under the refrigerator of the condominium I recently moved into."

"OK. So?"

"The condo used to belong to Dylan McCoy. That's who wrote that note, right? That's who you're waiting for?"

Kate put her hands in her pockets and leaned her hip against the railing, facing Paul. He could see her look of curiosity as she met his gaze. "So you know Dylan? Where'd he move to?"

Oh, God, Paul thought. *This isn't going to be easy.* He glanced over at the river, hoping it would give him strength.

"No. I didn't know Dylan." He paused before turning to her again. "Listen, do you have family here?"

"Wh—what? No. I'm visiting from, um, from out of town."

Once again he took in a deep breath and could see Kate was getting exasperated. "Look, there's no easy way to tell you. And God knows you shouldn't be hearing this from a stranger."

Kate's eyebrows furrowed. "Has…something happened?"

Paul began to roughly rub the back of his neck, hating himself for not having stayed put at his kitchen table. He composed himself quickly and leaned forward slightly, speaking softly. "I'm so sorry to be the one to tell you, but Dylan McCoy died just after Christmas. Heart attack or something, I'm not sure. God, it stinks that no one got word to you about it."

Kate stayed composed, her posture straight, but the single tear that streamed down her face told Paul that his news hit her hard.

"Oh." Kate looked down, discretely rubbed her gloved hand across her cheek and raised her head again stoically. "It was nice of you to come out here and let me know. You didn't have to do that."

Her voice was crisp, but Paul knew that was how she was keeping herself from losing it. He knew because he'd used the same tone and demeanor when he'd arrived at the hospital and met with the doctors about Ginny and Carlie. He knew that inside, Kate had to be falling apart.

⦵

Dylan had died. Kate had never had the chance to tell him she wanted to come back. She'd always been a stubborn, independent fool, and now look what it had cost her.

"God…," Kate whispered. She lowered her eyes again, focusing on her hands as she nervously played with the tips of her gloves. *Get your composure back, kiddo. This man is staring at you.*

A breeze blew her hair in her face and she quickly pulled it back, holding it as she once again made eye contact with the man in front of her. "I apologize. I…I wasn't expecting that his not showing up would be because he'd died. I'm a little in shock here." She smiled weakly and extended her hand. "Thank you…."

"Paul."

"Thank you, Paul. It was brave of you to come up here to—"

"No, no. Not brave at all. I…I don't know. I honestly didn't think you'd be here. I thought it was crazy for him to expect you to show up. But I figured I could use the walk anyw—"

"Why do you say that?" Kate interrupted. "Why did you think it was crazy for Dylan to expect me?" She was hurt that this stranger would make such an assumption; he didn't know either of them. He didn't know that every single day she'd fought the urge to come back to Dylan, stupid as her decision had been.

"I'm sorry…. The letters he'd written. Things just seemed so one-sided, like he knew it was a dream to think you'd come back, but yet he still believed you would."

"Letters? What letters?"

Paul sighed. He looked uncomfortable and seemed hesitant to continue. "When I moved in, I found a few things of his. Some photos of you from your college graduation and an envelope with a bunch of letters he wrote you but never sent. Kind of like he was keeping a journal, really."

"But his family...."

"I don't know. They'd cleaned out the place pretty quickly; they must have just not realized they'd left those things behind."

"No." Kate turned back to the railing and leaned out again, watching the waves and letting the cool breeze bite at her cheeks. "They probably left them behind because I'd left Dylan behind." Her voice was a whisper. "They wouldn't have wanted any reminders of me."

As she leaned against the railing again, it was obvious to Paul that she was in no hurry to leave. He had two choices: say a hasty good-bye and good luck...or show some compassion like his friends had to him. He knew from his own loss that talking was a way to start the healing process. Kate looked like she had no one to turn to. It was worth a shot.

"Tell me about him."

"What?" Kate gave a nervous laugh. "Look, you've been very kind, but—"

"I mean it. Tell me about him. I read letter after letter about how much he adored you and was so proud of you. Look at the note I gave you. He'd wanted to be here; he'd planned to be here."

Kate glanced over at Paul, her eyes filled with tears. "He was proud of me?"

Paul moved closer and mirrored her stance at the railing. "Yeah. You work for Findlay-Patterson, right?" She nodded. "I know that because he cut out articles with your name in them, and then he wrote you letters, asking you about what you'd accomplished. I'm sorry he never sent them to you."

"We'd sort of made a deal that he'd let me 'pursue my dreams' and not contact me. It was stupid." She paused, and Paul saw fresh tears stream down her face. "Really, really stupid."

"Those letters and things are yours," he offered. "Are you staying in town? I can bring them to you."

"Yeah. I'm at the bed and breakfast on Hanley, but I think I'm going to head back to Chicago tonight. I can't be here. There's nothing left here for me now. Even seeing that bicycle shop will break my heart."

"You mean 'Folks with Spokes'?"

Kate turned to him with a smile. "That was Dylan's pride and joy. He'd gotten a loan from his grandfather and bought the place just after graduation. He worked day and night." She sputtered a laugh. "I was ready to chuck my job in Chicago and move back here tomorrow if he'd shown up here and simply smiled at me. That's all it would have taken."

"I've been there. It was a good shop. They had lots of—" Tricycles, Paul remembered, but he stopped before he'd choke up. "They had lots to choose from." Paul had donated Carlie's tricycle as well as many of her toys to the church's preschool when he'd moved out of the house. "It's been closed since he died, though. I think the family wants to sell it."

"Really." Kate narrowed her eyes a little and then looked toward the water again, staying silent. Paul watched her and noticed how much she'd matured since that college photo. She was beautiful, smart, confident yet sensitive. And her eyes—so much like Ginny's. As she looked across the river, though, he saw specks of yellow mixed with the green. This wasn't Ginny. Paul knew that. His coworker's words began to echo in his mind. *You've got to let Ginny go. Allow yourself the opportunity to maybe find someone new.*

"How long have you lived in Marietta?" Kate's words broke into his thoughts.

"Um. Just over a month. But I only moved over here from Williamstown. I grew up there."

"And you work around here, too, I take it?"

"Yeah. I'm the principal at the high school there." He laughed. "Never a dull moment when you're surrounded by a few hundred teenagers."

"It is nice here, isn't it," Kate mused. "I guess I never gave it a chance. I just *had* to be a big-city girl for a while." Fresh tears formed along her lower lids.

"You can't regret your decision. Dylan loved you, but even he knew you had to do it. He wrote that so many times in his letters. He knew that if he'd forced you to stay, you would have been miserable together."

"So instead we were miserable apart," she choked out.

"I feel bad I never met the guy. Two small towns so close together; we'd probably crossed paths a million times."

"You would have liked him. Everybody did." Kate paused, a smile on her lips. "He was a good and honest man; never put on airs for anyone, never expected anyone to work harder than he did. If I'd stayed, we would have been married with a few kids by now."

"Kids are good. They ground you, make you realize what's really important."

Kate turned toward Paul. "You have kids, then, eh?"

He glanced back toward Williamstown and the part of his life that was gone forever. "No." *You've got to let Ginny go....* Paul straightened and slapped his hands on the railing, choosing to focus on Kate rather than himself. "Unless you count the three hundred kids in my school," he added with a half-hearted smile.

Kate gave a polite laugh, and then it was quiet again. "So, what made you move across the river? Needed some distance, even just a little bit?"

Paul sighed as he absently picked at a few loose chips of paint along the railing. "Yeah. I guess you could say that."

They both looked out over the water. On the grassy knoll on the Williamstown side of the river, a couple had wandered down to the water's edge. After throwing some small stones, as if making wishes upon them, the man wrapped his arm around the woman and she leaned into him, a single rose in her hand. They gave each other sweet kisses a few times, and then they turned back, holding hands as they strode up the hill to the road. *Let her go, Paul. It's time.*

A strong gust hit them, and Kate shivered. "Are we expecting another cold front tonight?" she asked.

"Sure does seem like it." Paul stepped back from the railing again and glanced at his watch; it was nearing four o'clock. "Hey, the afternoon's only going to get colder from here. It's probably best that we get indoors before this chill gets any worse."

Kate stammered uncomfortably. "Oh—of course. I'm sorry to have taken so much of your time. You were so sweet to come up here. Thank you. I guess I'd better—"

Let her go, Paul. Let Ginny go.

"Would you want to, I don't know, get a cup of coffee or something?" Paul asked hesitantly. "My place is on the way to a shop on King that we could go to. I could stop and get that packet of letters for you."

Kate looked at Paul for a long moment, studying him, and he simply stood there, his heart ready to open up for the first time in a year.

"Yeah. That'd be nice. I'd like that."

They turned and began to walk, side by side, toward Marietta…and new possibilities.

ABOUT THE AUTHORS

Alice Clayton attended University of Missouri, with an emphasis on Theater Arts. She now makes her home in South St Louis City, where she shares her life with her long time boyfriend Peter, and their children of the four legged variety. This is Alice's first novel. Her website is aliceclayton.com

Jennifer DeLucy grew up in the valley city of Scranton, Pennsylvania, where she developed an obsession with all things literary and musical thanks to the influence of an extroverted and creative family. While in Pennsylvania, Jennifer studied voice and had her first taste of professional writing as editor for a small organization. Jennifer moved to the Midwest in 2002, and she continues to pursue opportunities as an author and musician.

Nicki Elson first discovered her talent for writing when she faced the challenge of turning dry financial information into something understandable and interesting for her clients. Throughout her business career, effective writing has been an integral part of what she does. Nicki prefers, however, to lose herself in fiction writing, where she creates multidimensional, realistic characters and watches them react to the crazy situations she puts them in. Nicki currently resides in the suburbs of Chicago with her husband and two children.

ABOUT THE AUTHORS

Jessica McQuinn is a mom of two very active kids. They keep her busy running from activity to activity, but it is in those moments that she finds inspiration and has no problem pulling out a notebook to write down a few lines for her next story. Married for 20 years to her high school crush, Jessica lives in Utah with her family. Jessica has been writing all her life, but it wasn't until her kids started school that she decided to think that she could do it and actually share it with others. She hopes her readers you will enjoy her books as much as she has enjoyed writing them.

Victoria Michaels is a wife and mother of four who lives her life in what seems like a constant state of motion. Kids' sports, meetings, homework and general family fun take up twenty-seven hours of her day. In her thirty seconds of free time, Victoria likes to read, write and travel the country with her husband. She enjoys writing about love and laughter, two things that are central to her everyday life. If you would like to know more about what's coming next from Victoria, please check her out at victoriamichaels.net for updates, news and sneak peeks at future releases.

Alison Oburia has always had novel plots moving around in her head but has only recently begun to delve into getting those ideas down on paper. She's fortunate to have a husband and two sons who support her in her endeavors and constant possession of the family's computer as she writes late into the night. A former teacher, Alison now works as a consultant for two companies, which allows her to have a flexible schedule to write when the inspiration hits.